TulipTree review

FALL/WINTER 2019-2020
ISSUE #7

GENRE

TULIPTREE
PUBLISHING, LLC

Contents

Infinite Realities

Alexander Weinstein

WHEN WE FINALLY DISCOVERED THE PARALLEL-TIMELINE MOUSE, IT WAS sleeping in a universe so onionskin close to our own that it existed in a parallel cage in a parallel lab where a parallel Donnie and I were doing similar parallel-timeline experiments. I isolated the mouse on my monitor and dragged its timeline onto our present one. Then Donnie and I looked at our mouse sipping water from the feeder.

"Okay, let's do it," Donnie said, and I hit Enter.

We waited, wondered if the Earth would stop spinning, if matter would crack open, if alternate timelines would go spilling across the universe. But none of that happened. Instead the parallel-timeline mouse awoke inside the cage and sniffed his new universe. Then he crossed toward his present-timeline self, and the two mice put their noses together. Did they know they were the same mouse simply overlapped from different timelines? Were they behaviorally different mice? Might this shed some light on the whole nature-versus-nurture debate? Who knew? We were opening the champagne.

DONNIE HAD FIRST ASKED if I could write program for transdimensionality back in college. We'd been smoking some heavy-duty Indica, and I'd had a vision of a spider's web of infinite timelines, the program's layers as user-friendly as Photoshop. Yeah, I told him, I could do it, but he was the scientist—it was up to him to figure out the hard quantum shit, like traversing string theory and locating multiple realities. Sure enough, eight years later, he did.

We celebrated all week. Donnie splurged on expensive rum, and I broke out my top-shelf bud. We repeated experiments, recorded the transdimensional mouse, daydreamed about the Nobel Prize, and for a while it was high times in that lab. Donnie worked on wave/particle equations, leaving me to mess around with new programming. I worked to isolate anything we had biology on: a single strand of fur from Donnie's golden retriever let me track infinite parallel versions of his dog throughout the multiverse. Things were going great, but as we broke through the fabric of reality, all I could think about was Erin cheating on me with that woman at her stupid teachers' conference. I took bong hits after work and watched YouTube clips of cats riding skateboards to keep from dwelling on it.

We'd met at the campus Film Club three years earlier, and when I first saw Erin it was like we were two alternate-timeline mice finally together in the same cage. I invited her back to my place to smoke a bowl, and we made out until early morning. By winter we were spending every day together, and by the end of the school year she invited me to move into her apartment. It was tight, but we made it work, pulling tubes and watching dumb horror flicks late into the night. There wasn't room for my equipment, so I worked on programming at the lab, cracking the codes of time and space while Erin studied education reform at home. Then her dissertation year started and she stopped puffing altogether. I'd crawl into bed after work, ready to tell her about our latest breakthrough, but she'd just take my hand in hers, sniff it, and tell me I better not touch her with my resin fingers. As if that wasn't bad enough, after six months of no sex, she went and cheated on me with some rando. So, yeah, I was super bummed when I should've been celebrating the mouse successes.

Erin was in bed reading when I came home from the two hundredth lab test. I went into the kitchen and looked for food, but dinner was already cleaned up. "Any leftovers?"

"Didn't make enough for two," she said, and looked up. "Please tell me you didn't just walk into the kitchen with your boots on."

"Shit, sorry." I took off my wet boots and put them on the shoe rack, then grabbed some paper towels and mopped up the muddy prints. I microwaved a burrito, which started another fight. Why did I eat junk all the time? Why did it matter if we weren't having sex? Maybe it'd be sexy if I got a job. Um, I had an actual job; I was doing groundbreaking freaking science. Playing with mice for two hundred bucks a week didn't constitute *groundbreaking science*. Well, maybe if she asked me about transdimensionality or spooky action at a distance she might know how freaking awesome our discoveries were. Was I seriously rolling a joint right now? Why the fuck not? Then she was shutting our bedroom door, and I was alone, puffing really good ganj out the kitchen window. I knocked on her door to ask if she wanted a hit, and she told me to start looking for a new apartment.

So, yeah, I was hurt and heartbroken. I wanted our old timeline back: a reality where we wrestled on the couch, made love every night, and when the munchies hit, bundled into parkas and trekked it to the Shell station for cheese puffs. And no, it wasn't morally right, or well thought out, or even a plan—I was just really high and had access to Erin's hair. Seriously, I wasn't trying to fuck up everyone's lives. I only wanted to know if somewhere in the universe there was an Erin who still loved me.

AMONG THE NINE MILLION things that could've gone wrong: I could've wrecked the space-time continuum; the Earth could've become a black hole; the program could've glitched and an alternate Erin would've been trapped between parallel realities in a netherworld where particle trash and hungry ghosts passed her forever. But what I was hoping, when I dragged one of her timelines onto mine, was that particles would instinctively know how to make room for other particles, that a parallel-timeline concert was also happening at the Blind Pig, and that Erin would find herself there, seamlessly dancing, without ever knowing the difference. So, I closed my eyes and hit Enter.

By the time I got to the club, Erin was by the stage. Her hair was longer and her shoulders weren't slumped from typing, and when she turned and saw me making my way through the crowd, I had that same fluttering feeling in my heart like the first time I'd seen her at the Film Club.

"Good band, huh?" I yelled.

"Yeah!" she yelled back. "Did you see the first one?"

"No! It's loud in here!"

"Want to go smoke a bowl?"

"Sure!"

Alongside the other smokers, we got high in the alleyway for the first time in over a year. Erin told me about playing guitar in a dub-folk band and how she web-designed to pay the bills. I told her about the mouse experiments, and she didn't make fun of me. Instead she said, "Are you kidding? That's fucking incredible!" and looked at me with such curiosity that it was hard not to blush. I stared at the firebird tattoo on her neck instead; tattoos were something my timeline Erin hated. The bowl was cashed and she dug around in her pocket.

"Should've brought more," she said. "We can puff at my place if you want. It's in Chelsea, but I can give you a ride."

No, you can't, I thought, looking at the garage across the street.

"I have to finish an experiment tonight," I said. "How about tomorrow? Want to go for a walk at the arb?"

"I free up at four."

"Meet you by the gates?"

"It's a date," she said, and leaned forward, giving me a quick kiss. The sudden softness of her mouth against mine was the most incredible feeling I'd had all year. I stood there, watching as she turned, thinking how there was a timeline where we were still in the alleyway making out, another where she was touring with a dub-folk band, and yet another where she'd soon leave the club and call the police about her missing car. *Shit*. I hurried back to the lab, highlighted her parallel self, and returned her to her own reality. Then I took out a pad and wrote down every detail I could remember: the sound of her voice, the warmth of her lips against mine, what it felt like to be wanted again. When I was done, I shut off the lights and went home to our apartment, where Erin was asleep, her own note on the kitchen table telling me to crash on the couch.

I HADN'T EXPECTED TO fall in love again so quickly. But at work the next day, I told Donnie I needed to go home early, and before leaving I isolated the alternate Erin, dragged her timeline over my own, and hit Enter. Six hours later, we were parked outside the empty lab, making out in my car while snow came down heavy against the steamed-up windows. Then I let her into the building, showed her the mice, and finally highlighted her timeline and dragged her back over hers. We kissed one last time, the whole universe feeling alive; then I hit Enter and there was just me, alone in the lab with the small lights of my computer blinking and our two mice sleeping tightly against each other.

So, I did what I knew had to happen in this reality. I called Donnie.

"*Are you totally insane?* Like fucking sociopathic?" Donnie asked when he arrived at the lab. He was still in pajama pants, his hair a mess, wearing a T-shirt with Einstein on it. "You brought another human into our reality?"

"Twice," I said.

"Do you have any fucking clue how dangerous that is?"

"Kinda."

"Kinda?" Donnie said. "*Kinda?* You could've imploded multiple realities."

"Precisely," I said. "Take a moment and process that. It worked!" And I kept reminding Donnie that the first human tests had worked, until he relaxed enough to stop panicking. I took the bottle of rum from the file cabinet and poured us two large tumblers while I told him about how Erin and I had walked together through the arb, the branches covered in a light dusting of snow, how the softness of her jacket had rubbed against mine, and her voice had been buoyant, how she was completely different from my Erin, who treated me as though I was an intruder in her joy.

"Can you speed up this story a bit? Like, to the part where you don't create an irreparable tear in time and space?"

"I'm just saying she was real in this universe. Like a perfect but better version of my Erin. She took the joint we were smoking from my hand as naturally as if we'd been together for years. Seriously, we should be celebrating."

"I'll celebrate once I know you haven't fucked up the multiverse," Donnie said. All the same, he took a long sip of his rum and sat down at his desk across from me.

"It was incredible," I told Donnie. "We were standing by the Huron River, the snow falling, her body buzzing against mine, sunlight making everything sparkly with winter, and she told me I was amazing. We kissed like it was the first time, the falling snow shimmering and beautiful around us."

"Wow, that's really fucking great, man. You risked imploding the universe for a make-out session with your girlfriend. Please tell me you didn't inform her she was from another reality."

"Well, I showed her the mouse video and told her she was the mouse and she freaked. 'You quantum kidnapped me?' she said. I tried to explain that the other her had cheated on me and we hadn't had sex for a year, but—"

"*Are you joking?*" Donnie said, and got up again. "That means there's a person in another dimension who knows they've transcended realities."

"I figured it was the only right thing to do, especially since we were making out. But once she heard about the other her, she demanded to see herself."

"*Fuck.*"

"Don't worry, they didn't meet. We just sat for a while in the car snooping on my place. It was getting dark and the snow was falling heavier, and Erin just watched my Erin as she worked on her computer. She wanted to know if she ever did anything else besides work on her dissertation, like play guitar, or smoke weed, or go to concerts. I told her she didn't. 'Shit, so I'm super lame in this reality," she said. Then she said she didn't want to mess with my Erin's head like I'd messed with hers, she just wanted to go back to her own universe."

I'd felt awful as I drove her back through downtown. I'd never meant to kidnap her or mess things up so badly. Ann Arbor was lit up with Christmas lights that hadn't been taken down yet, and it was super cozy and romantic with couples walking along Main Street holding hands. Erin was looking out her window at the guy on the corner wearing a wolf mask, playing violin in the falling snow.

"I still don't get it," she said. "If you were trying to get even with *her,* you could've cheated with someone in your own reality. Why'd you kidnap me?"

"Because I never thought of it as cheating," I said, "or kidnapping. I just thought of it as finding another part of you that still loved me in a subconscious string-theory kind of way. Seriously, I don't want anyone else, I only want you."

"Wait, she fucking bought that?" Donnie said.

"Bought what? It's the truth, I'm in love with her."

Which was what I'd told her in the car. We were stopped by a red light, with the pedestrians all passing, and she looked over at me and said, "Explain to me again why the other me isn't making out with you in this reality."

"I don't know," I said. "Maybe because I smoke too much weed?"

"Well, that's stupid. You should know that other me is missing out because you're really hot," she said. And then we were kissing again, our hands all over each other, until the guy behind us was honking because the light had turned green.

"So, moral of the story is your girlfriend from another dimension thinks you're hot?" Donnie said.

"No, you're missing the point. Erin agreed with me. She said it was fucked up to make out together in a universe where the other her also existed, but that she'd be willing to keep seeing me if I came to her. Donnie, I can be the human test subject now. Put me in her timeline and bring me back. I'll give you reports. You know, for science."

"Uh-huh. Since when have you been remotely interested in the actual science of any of this?"

"I'm totally interested in science. Look, I took notes." I showed him my journal from the first meeting with Erin.

"What is this, a love letter?"

"All right, you're the one who knows how to take lab notes. That's what I'm saying: use me as your lab rat." And then, knowing the scientist in him could never say no, I added, "You *really* don't want to run tests?"

Donnie took a long drink of his rum before looking at me. "What if I can't bring you back?"

"That's not going to happen. You know how good my programs are. The experiment worked. The mice prove it, Erin proves it. This is what we wanted all along—the ability to travel through multiple dimensions. Seriously, we're talking about the Nobel Prize. Let's just try it, *for science's sake.*"

"Luke," Donnie said. He sat down across from me and tilted his glass in warning. "You're an incredible programmer, but sometimes you're also a fucking idiot. Maybe you were successful in our universe, but who knows what damage you caused in that other dimension. So, if we do this, you need to tell me everything from now on. No more lies about where you're going, no secrets. I'm going to need to know if anything in that world goes wrong."

"Of course." I clinked his glass. "Here's to infinite possibilities."

WE STARTED WITH A couple hours. Donnie dragged me over Erin's lake house, hit Enter, and suddenly the lab was gone and I was outside Erin's house in the cold. It had snowed in her reality, and everything looked silvery and beautiful, the lake covered in a layer of snow, the branches all heavy with white. I walked to the front door, reached out and knocked, and there was Erin, opening the door in fuzzy slippers.

"I was wondering if you were coming. Well, welcome to my reality."

Erin's lake house was a one-bedroom cabin that had a living room with a sliding glass door to a porch overlooking the lake. On the floor by the window was a steaming cup of tea next to her guitar. I took off my shoes by the door, and Erin and I sat cross-legged on the warm wooden floor facing each other.

"I found the *other* you on Facebook." She held up my profile pic on her phone. There was my stupid cowlick, my jawline, my eyes, and my goofy smile. But this guy was way more buff, and he was standing beside a frizzy-haired woman and two boys who looked exactly like me. He was wearing a tank top that said "God Bless America."

"I look like I've never smoked a joint in my life."

"Want me to friend you?"

"Please don't."

"Check this one out." Erin swiped to an old photo of me at a weightlifting competition, my meaty hand on a beefcake dude, both of us giving a thumbs-up.

"Okay, that's super creepy."

"Kinda like if somebody grabbed you and put you in their timeline without asking?"

"I'm so sorry about that. Can you forgive me?"

"Yeah," Erin said, putting her phone away and placing her hands against my thighs as she leaned toward me. "I think I can do that."

* * *

DONNIE BROUGHT ME BACK to the lab and I gave him notes on traversing timelines, let him take EKG readings and draw blood samples for interdimensional radioactivity. I asked him to increase my next visit to three hours, then five, and soon I was at Erin's lake house most of the day. We'd make love and smoke joints, and she'd practice new songs for me. There was no TV at the lake, so we did other things, like hiking and cooking and making plans to go kayaking once it got warmer. Being with her let me see how much of a slacker I'd been in my own universe. I envisioned that other me, slumped on the couch, my feet on the coffee table littered with roaches and beer bottles, playing video games all night, and I felt embarrassed for the person I'd become.

That evening when I returned to our small apartment, Erin was in the bedroom in front of her computer. I cleaned up the kitchen and did push-ups in the living room, and we didn't fight or argue about not having sex, I just surprised her by cooking dinner, and Erin was happy to have the time to write. She'd left her earrings on the kitchen table. They were a small gift I'd found at the Tibetan shop downtown when we first started dating—two turquoise teardrops. Seeing them, I suddenly envisioned a timeline where Erin was gone from my life, taking her earrings and everything else with her when she left.

"Hey," I said, standing in the doorway of our bedroom. Erin turned from the computer, annoyed, and I took a deep breath. "I know I've been smoking weed and playing video games all the time and probably haven't been that interesting to live with."

"Okay," she said.

"And I know you probably felt really alone because of it. And I'm sorry. I haven't been much of a boyfriend. I was hoping weed would help, because we used to laugh and have fun, but I was wrong. So, I just want you to know that I'd like to do other things with you, like take walks, or cook together, or . . . well . . . whatever you want to do. I just want to be with you."

Erin took a deep breath and looked at me. Then she got up and crossed the room and gave me a hug. I felt the warmth of her body against mine, and though I'd been holding her at the lake that afternoon, this Erin felt completely new.

"I'm glad you're saying this," she said into my ear, "but it's going to take time for me to believe you. I need to actually see you making changes."

And though we didn't kiss, just stood in the light of our bedroom, I could feel her love again, and when she let me go, instead of pulling tubes or turning on PlayStation, I decided to do some more push-ups in the living room and get into shape like that other me in Erin's world.

THINGS GOT BETTER. I'D see Erin at the lake house during the day and spend evenings with the other Erin at night. We cooked dinner at home and joked like we used to, and though we hadn't kissed yet, we hugged more. Meanwhile, in that other reality, Erin and I spent hours naked in bed pleasuring each other. Afterward, we lay together like new lovers, talking about a future where we'd use Donnie's discovery as a travel agency to teleport us to a multiverse in Paris or Morocco. But it was also true that life was getting complicated. Now that things were thawing at home, Erin was sending me romantic text messages that I couldn't answer for hours. I asked Donnie to field them for me.

"Sexting isn't in my job description," he said. "You know what is? Quantum physics research. You should try it sometime."

"Please. I'll write you notes you can use. Just text her back so she thinks I'm here."

And maybe everything could've worked out, the four of us all functioning together across multiple dimensions—Donnie fielding texts for me, Erin and me happy at the lake house while the other us healed our past in the present—if only reality hadn't started getting weird. Like how Erin was humming a dub-folk melody while she worked on her dissertation, the very same song the other Erin had been playing for me earlier that day. Or how she began talking about getting a tattoo, a firebird on her forearm. And then there was the night when she woke me. I was still sleeping on the couch, the moonlight coming through the living room window, and for a moment in my half-asleep state I thought I saw the frozen lake outside and couldn't remember whether I was at the lake house or our apartment.

"Luke?" Erin said from the doorway. I blinked my eyes and saw her guitar in the corner of the room.

"Yeah?" I said, rubbing my eyes.

"Can you come back to bed and hold me?"

So, I got up from the couch, and there was no sliding glass doorway, no lake outside, no guitar in the corner, just the snowy windows of our small apartment, and our bedroom where I was finally being allowed back under the covers. I crawled beneath the blankets beside her, and Erin wrapped her arms around me.

"I had an awful dream," she said. "We were at this weird lake house smoking weed and we were so happy and in love, but you were cheating on me. I was playing this sad song for you on guitar, about the moon and my heart, and then you got up from bed and kissed me, and"—she started crying—"and I realized how much I've been missing you." She put her hand against my face.

"You dreamt about a lake house?"

"Luke," Erin said, wiping away her tears, "I'm sorry I cheated on you. I was sad and felt disconnected, and you didn't seem to notice, you were just smoking weed all the time, and I thought you were becoming someone different . . . and I didn't like the new you."

"I understand," I said. "But what about the lake house in your dream?"

"Who cares, it was just a dumb house, that's not the important part. What's important is the feeling I had of missing you and loving each other—I want that again."

"I want that, too," I said, and we kissed for what felt like the first time in over a year.

"Luke," she said, pulling away to look at me. "What's wrong? It's like you're somewhere else."

"I'm right here," I said.

"There's just this hollow feeling—it's awful. Like this morning, in class, I felt all this anger toward you, like you were cheating on me. Tell me the truth: Are you seeing someone else?"

"Just you," I said.

And then we were kissing again, our bodies warm against each other like the first time after the Film Club, her hands slipping beneath my shirt as we pulled each other's clothes off. "I haven't told you," Erin whispered, "but sometimes when you're at work, I can feel you touching me. Your lips against the back of my neck, your hands on me." She took my face and kissed me again. "I've been missing you so much. I'm sorry for what's been happening; I want us back." And we pressed our bodies together like we'd done at the lake house, the two of us feeling completely familiar and totally foreign from who we'd once been.

I KNEW I SHOULD mention Erin's dream to Donnie—it was the kind of thing he needed to know—but the next morning, Erin and I woke up and made love again, and when she asked if I could skip work, I called Donnie and told him I'd be late.

Donnie was pissed when I got to the lab. "Dude, I don't know what's going on with you. First you complain about not having enough time in the parallel dimension, now you're showing up late? I need you *here*. We're totally falling behind on the mouse experiments." It was true. For all practical purposes, I'd been gone from the lab for weeks; progress on the next stage was slowing.

"Don't we need more data?" I asked.

"I've got tons of data. Seriously, you've got to stop messing around with your second girlfriend and get back to work."

"Oh, man," I said. "That's really going to mess things up for us." I sat there wondering if there was a reality where both Erins would fall in love and we could have a deeply meaningful threesome. I asked Donnie what he thought. "It'd be amazing, right? Though, I guess it might feel kind of narcissistic. Still, if you *didn't* want to hook up with yourself, does that mean you secretly have low self-esteem? What do you think? Would you ever make out with yourself?"

"Luke, what the fuck's wrong with you? I need you here in the lab with me to write new programs. We've got a serious situation on our hands. Have you even been reading the notes I left you about wave temporality and the dangers of collapsing timelines?"

"Um—"

"Okay, we're cutting you back to three hours."

Donnie was, of course, right, but mostly I was thinking about how hard it'd be not to see the other Erin. Plus, I knew I had to tell her about sleeping with this-reality Erin, but Erin just jumped on me when I appeared at the lake house, and we stripped each other naked and made love instead.

It was deep winter, the light already gone, and we lay in her bed, the candles flickering against the walls, watching the sun disappear behind the pines at the far end of the lake. Her hand was against my chest, her touch reminding me of all the mornings we'd woken up in bed together in our other reality, back when we'd find each other beneath the blankets, feeling as though we were the luckiest people alive.

"I've been feeling strange," Erin told me, her face highlighted by the glow of the candle. "It's like I'm living these two different lives that can never match up. I can't text, can't call, can only wait around for you to show up, and then you have to leave whenever your lab buddy calls you back. And meanwhile, the real you—the one in this reality— is just some married beefcake dude. What's that even mean? Is that secretly the real you?"

"No. This is the real me."

"Well, this setup sucks. I don't want you living with some other me, sleeping there, eating together; I want you here, with me, in my reality. You said you liked this me better, right? Can't you break up with that other me and move into my timeline?"

"Well . . . I mean . . . I've got my family in the other world, and my job."

"You could still visit them. Get a new job here."

I lay in bed wondering if that could work. Could I go back and visit my parents for the holidays, catch up with old buddies? And what about the other Erin, the one I had photos and memories of, the one who'd been sending me happy texts again, my lover who I was falling back in love with?

A small jewelry tree stood on the dresser, and hanging from it was the pair of turquoise earrings from the Tibetan shop that I'd bought Erin.

"Where'd you get those?" I asked. I got out of bed and looked at them. They had the same small fleck of tarnish in the silver, precisely the flaw in the pair I'd given Erin.

"Didn't you give me . . . Actually, let me see them," Erin said. I brought the earrings to her. "I can't remember where I got them, but they're really nice."

I didn't mention the earrings to Donnie when I got back to the lab, but that night I searched and couldn't find them anywhere. "Stop looking for things and come kiss me," Erin said, wrapping her arms around me. And though I wanted to double-check the bathroom cabinet, she pulled me into the bedroom where we made love again.

The next morning, Erin asked me about her favorite coffee mug. We'd gotten it a year ago when we drove cross-country to see her parents. "The one we got from Montana with the big heart on it?" she said, rummaging through the cabinets.

I couldn't find it until that afternoon when I went to get water at the lake house and saw the mug in Erin's cabinet. "Do you recognize this?" I asked.

"Nope. Maybe somebody left it when I had a party."

I didn't say anything, but the next time I visited her, my PlayStation was in her living room. "Why'd you bring this?" she asked me. "I don't even have a TV."

I knew I had to tell Donnie what was happening, but I also knew if I did, he'd stop me from going back to Erin's reality altogether. I figured I could take my own notes, keep track of things for another couple weeks, figure out how to come clean with everyone, and maybe discover a happy solution for us all, but it was becoming harder to keep track of my timelines. In one reality I lay in bed with Erin, looking out our small window at the snowy street, remembering how we'd promised to go kayaking only to realize that wasn't in this reality at all. Next I was lying with Erin at the lake house, her room awash with the yellow glow of candlelight, and she was telling me about how she'd been getting interested in education reform, directly quoting passages from the dissertation my other Erin was working on. And then, late one afternoon, we were standing on her snow-dusted deck together, watching the light wane across the lake, and she was remembering the movie we'd seen on the night we'd met at the Film Club, a memory that was totally not hers.

A couple of geese were honking on the far side of the water, the first returns from their winter pilgrimage, and they floated along the defrosted edge, the sky darkening with evening. Somewhere, in another timeline, geese were probably returning to this same lake. Were they the same geese? Did they think the same goose thoughts? Was the lake house my future? That's when we heard the other Erin banging on the front door.

"Open this fucking door!"

"Who is that?" Erin said, turning from the lake and sliding open the glass.

"Luke! Erin! I know you're in there."

"Oh my god, that sounds like me," Erin said.

Then I was back in the lab looking at Donnie. "What the fuck, man?"

"Sorry," Donnie said. "She came by to surprise you and saw the sexting notes on my desk. I had to tell her the truth. She pretty much forced me to send her there."

"*What?* Put me back!"

"Listen," Donnie said. "This whole thing was not okay. Like not for science, or you, or Erin, or me—"

"Just send me back for a couple minutes so I can explain things."

"What's wrong with you? You cheated on two versions of your girlfriend. Neither of them is going to want to talk to you right now. You need to give them space. Go home, smoke dope, get some sleep, come back tomorrow."

What choice did I have? The moment I clicked Enter, Donnie brought me right back to the lab. So, I walked home to our small apartment, where I could see traces of Erin in the moments before she'd left to surprise me. There was our bed, where last night we'd fantasized about a summer trip to Barcelona. There were the dishes from her lunch on the table, and drafts of her dissertation by her computer—all glimpses of the life we'd been rebuilding before I'd ruined it. My PlayStation was gone, lost in an alternate dimension. All I had was some weed in the closet, and a six-pack I'd picked up on the way home. So, I opened a bottle and loaded the bong for myself and got high alone for the last time in what had once been our reality.

THE DOOR OPENED EARLY next morning. I blinked awake, the whole world hurting, to find the two of them standing in the morning light looking like sisters. Lake House Erin surveyed our messy living room with the empty bottles, rolling papers, and ashy coffee table, then looked back at red-eyed, hungover me, seeing me for the first time the way my Erin had seen me for the past year. "Get out of bed," my Erin said before shutting the door behind her so I could get dressed.

When I finally sat across from the two Erins at the kitchen table, the world was swimming behind my eyes. "I can't believe you lied to me," Lake House Erin said and looked to the other her. "Last night I finally got to know myself, and I actually like who I am. I'm a good person, Luke, and you helped me stab myself in the back." She reached out and put her hand on Erin's. "I'm sorry."

"It's not your fault; that's just what he does. He's selfish and fucked up," Erin said. Then she looked at me. "I was mad at you both, but now that I've had time alone with myself, I realize I'm just mad that I chose you again."

"But I love you. Isn't that, like, an even better testament of my love, that I love all the different versions of you?"

"Luke," my Erin said, "the only reason we're here is to tell you that this—us—is over."

"Can we talk about this? It doesn't have to end this way; there's infinite realities. What about the reality where all of us love one another?"

"We're going back to the lab," Erin said. "Erin's returning to her reality and I'm staying here in a reality without you. So, take your clothes, take your fucking bong, and get your stuff out of here. When I get back, I want the front door locked with your key under the mat."

"Where am I supposed to go?"

"Some alternate dimension, a parallel universe, I don't care, just any reality that doesn't include me."

I looked to Lake House Erin. "I guess you were right about me coming to your reality."

"No way," she said. "You're manipulative, self-centered, and toxic, and you helped me lie to myself. That's seriously fucked up. I never want to see you again." Then she got up from the table, and I watched them leave the apartment, holding each other's hands as they disappeared from my reality forever.

I took a shower, my head still pounding. Then I gathered my clothes and packed a box with my video games and dope before calling Donnie to ask for help moving my stuff.

"Are you joking? I'm here with both Erins. They told me about the melding—the coffee mug, the earrings, your PlayStation—didn't you think that might be important? Like, *crucial fucking information?* I can't help you move your shit, I'm a little busy trying to solve a quantum entanglement catastrophe that might implode reality."

"I'm sorry."

"*Sorry?* Dude, you were supposed to give me data, not lie to me so you could have sex with your alternate-reality girlfriend."

"I know. I'll do better in the future."

"Are you high? You're off the project. The passcode for the lab is changed. Don't come back here." Then the connection went dead.

Everything Donnie said was true: I'd betrayed our work together, betrayed our friendship, betrayed both Erins, broken the fabric of reality, and possibly fucked up the multiverse irreversibly; there was nothing to do but call my parents and tell them I needed a place to stay. And maybe it was at that moment when I finally saw clearly that the person I was in this timeline was just a self-centered, lying piece of crap who'd messed up everyone's reality, including my own.

In the end, Donnie was able to save our realities and fix the multiverse, and I moved back home and got a sales job at the Apple store. I saw Donnie on the news last Christmas, his video already gone viral, the two small mice meeting each other again, their pink noses touching. There was Donnie with his new assistant, a guy who looked exactly like me, just more clean-cut and trustworthy. The YouTube clip already has more than a billion views, and the world is soon going to become way more complicated. Maybe in a dozen years I'll have access to those programs I once wrote, and I'll be able to return to the night when I left our apartment drunk, stoned, and stupid enough to search for another Erin. I'll tell myself to go home, to stop smoking so much weed, and to try to fix our relationship instead. Who knows if I'll listen, but I can at least try. Because I know there are countless timelines where I'm someone good, parallel universes where I make the right choices and no one gets hurt, infinite realities where I'm a better human being. And maybe, if I try hard enough, one of those realities can also be this one.

The Bad Guy

P. Jo Anne Burgh

THE JURY'S BEEN OUT SINCE YESTERDAY. KEVIN'S LAWYER—THE INFAMOUS
Henry P. R. Murdoch, the one with all those commercials on late-night
television—says the longer they're out, the better. God, I hope he's
right.

The closing arguments still ring in my ears. The prosecutor
arguing that Kevin murdered a young Hispanic man in cold blood, a
boy who didn't deserve to die just because he had brown skin and bad
judgment. Murdoch insisting it was self-defense, that Kevin was
standing his ground, protecting his home and his family. That what he
did was commendable. Brave. Even honorable.

Not that the jury heard any of this from my brother. Kevin didn't
take the stand. Criminal defendants almost never do, Murdoch
informed us when we asked. It doesn't mean anything bad when they
don't testify, he said. It's their constitutional right.

So, Kevin never faced a single question about what he thought
or what he saw or why he pulled the trigger at all, much less three
times. Marcel Luciano—the other kid who was there that night, the
one who didn't end up dead—he's the one who told what happened
when he and Ricardo Gomez turned around in my parents' living room
and saw the streetlight glinting off the barrel of my brother's gun. The
jury was left to speculate about what went through Kevin's mind when
he came up the stairs and saw Luciano yanking the flat-screen
television off the wall, and Gomez yelled that he had a knife.

As it turned out, Ricardo Gomez was lying. There was no knife—just a broken-off half of a plastic ruler, hidden under his sweatshirt. But it would have looked like a knife, Murdoch told the jury. He held the ruler under his expensive suit coat the way Luciano said Gomez had, and two jurors nodded.

Unfortunately for Ricardo Gomez, my brother wasn't lying when he yelled at Gomez to stop where he was or he'd be sorry. Luciano, who'd flung himself facedown on the rug and never moved until the police arrived, got immunity on a whole host of charges in exchange for his testimony about how Gomez panicked and ran and Kevin ran after him, yelling at him to stop and shooting when he didn't.

Three times, Kevin fired. Three times, he hit his target. The coroner testified Gomez was dead before he reached the sidewalk.

One shot might have been reasonable force—*might*, Murdoch said. Even that was no slam-dunk since the kid had been trying to get away. But when Kevin kept shooting even after Gomez fell . . . a jury might think Kevin really did want to kill the kid, not just stop him.

Not that I would ever entertain such an idea. Not even in the darkest corners of my mind.

KEVIN WAS BORN TO be a cop. I still remember him toddling around the house, red curls in disarray from his nap, wearing nothing but Pull-Ups and carrying an ancient metal cap pistol with no caps. *Sheriff McCormick*, we called him, and we laughed when he wrinkled up his round freckled face, waved his cap pistol, and barked, "Put 'em up!" Sometimes we wouldn't put 'em up, and then Kevin would aim at us and yell, "Pow! Pow! Pow!" I was already in the junior high drama club by that time, so I knew how to die a dramatic death that would satisfy my baby brother, but my father was Kevin's favorite target. He'd clutch his chest and lurch around the room, moaning and wailing, until suddenly his eyes would go wide and he'd stop in mid-wail, frozen until he fell to the carpet in a heap, right in front of Kevin. My little brother would nudge him with one pudgy bare foot. When Dad didn't move, Kevin would look up with a big smile. His eyes would shine with satisfaction as he crowed, "Got the bad guy!"

More than anything, my little brother wanted to protect and serve. When kids fought on the playground, he was the one yelling, "Break it up!" in as deep a voice as a ten-year-old can manage. He enjoyed being doted on by three older sisters, but he'd have traded us in a heartbeat for Colin Callahan's oldest brother, a rookie on the city police force who wore the uniform and carried a gun and walked with a swagger that let the bad guys know who was in charge.

Kevin was a junior the night his dream came to an end. It was the homecoming game against West Catholic. Short, stocky Kevin wasn't built for speed, but he could catch almost any throw, doggedly protecting the ball until he could hurl it to a faster teammate. The West Catholic kicker sent the ball sailing far, far down the field, farther than anybody'd expected. Kevin and half a dozen other boys dove for it, a tangle of arms and legs and helmets. Typical football melee. No big deal.

Until Coach Moreno blew his whistle and ran out to the field. The players parted, and from where we sat in the bleachers, I could see Kevin lying on the bright green grass. Dad and I sprang to our feet, making our way down to the field even before we really knew what was going on. My husband Bob stayed in the stands to calm Mom and Angie; luckily, Michelle was off at college, because she can get hysterical if a car wash malfunctions. By the time Dad and I got to the edge of the field, they were loading Kevin onto a stretcher, and we followed him to the locker room to wait together for the ambulance.

Shattered, the doctor said after the x-rays. I don't remember all the details, but the gist of it was that while Kevin would definitely walk and might even run a little bit, his football days were finished. "What about his future?" Mom asked. "He wants to be a cop."

The doctor pretended to look at the chart. After a minute, he met our eyes. "It's hard to say right now," he said. "It'll depend how the knee heals." Years later, I asked a friend who was a physical therapist, and she told me gently that from what I'd described, Kevin's career as a police officer ended on that football field. He never had a chance after that.

Not that he didn't try. My little brother is nothing if not tenacious. Bull-headed, actually, but "tenacious" sounds more like someone who uses common sense. From the second they took the cast off, he was trying to work the knee. "Hey, hold still. I gotta put the splint on," said Omar, the cast-and-splint guy at the orthopedic surgeon's office, but Kevin paid him no attention. He just clenched his teeth and started trying to bend his knee.

"Kev, maybe you should wait until the doctor says it's okay," I suggested. Mom and Dad echoed my comment as they perched on the plastic chairs in the corner of the examining room.

Kevin ignored us. He'd gotten out of his plaster prison, and he was ready to get back to work. Over the next several months, one or another of us drove him to physical therapy three times a week. At home, he turned the basement into a workout room, and he spent evenings sweating over his exercises. No academic homework had ever captured my brother's attention the way his PT assignments did.

Which was why it was so strange to walk into the house one day and see him sitting at the kitchen table doing nothing. "What's up?" I asked. He didn't answer, didn't even acknowledge me. I eased my increasing bulk into a chair, wincing as the baby delivered a sound kick under my ribs. "This kid's got your kick," I said.

"I don't have any kick," he muttered. "I don't have nothing."

"What are you talking about?" He didn't answer. "Kevvy. Talk to me. What's going on?"

He looked up. His blue eyes glistened. "Jimmy says . . . this is as good as it's gonna get." Jimmy was his physical therapist. A Vietnam vet with two missing fingers, Jimmy accepted no excuses for not working to the utmost. He and Kevin got along just fine.

"Oh, sweetie, I'm sorry." I reached over and laid a hand on his arm. "But how can he be sure? It's only been—what, seven months?"

"Almost eight," said Kevin, his gaze dropping to the table top. "Jimmy says by this point, what you got is what you got. Might change a little bit one way or the other, but basically, if it's not back by now, it's never gonna be."

"Well, that sucks." I was hoping for a smile in response, but he didn't look up. "What does he think about the pain? Is it going to get better?"

"Maybe, maybe not. Doesn't matter. He says I'm never gonna run again. Not the way I'll need to on the force."

I realized then that it wasn't losing senior year football that had Kevin so upset. He was looking a lot further down the road. "I'm sorry, Kevvy," I said. I rubbed his arm, but if he noticed, he gave no sign. "What if you got a new physical therapist? One who had some different exercises?"

His head shot up. "That's what I'm gonna do," he said with a touch of heat. "I still got a year before I have to take my physical. If I keep working, I bet I can get it good enough."

"I bet you can." I squeezed his hand. My little brother wasn't a quitter. One way or another, by sheer grit, he'd get himself on the force.

Except he didn't—at least, not the way he wanted to be, as a cop on the street. Bob had a friend who had a friend, and the friend's friend did what he could, but in the end, Kev just couldn't do it. Kevin never said a word, but Bob's friend said when he climbed the wall and jumped down on the other side, his knee gave out and he ended up crumpled on the ground, gasping with the pain. The officers in charge tried to help him up, but he shook them off and got himself to his feet and finished the course. The friend said nobody'd ever seen anything like it, but . . .

"You could get a job as a security guard," Mom said as she passed the potatoes at Sunday dinner a few days later.

Kevin scowled. "I'm not gonna be some stupid rent-a-cop," he said. "I'll figure out something else." The *something else* ended up being a position as a police dispatcher while he attended classes in criminal justice at the local community college, which would have been a great idea except for the number of students who were either police officers already or were preparing to be. Rubbing shoulders with people who were living the life he was supposed to have was hard on Kevin. As a dispatcher, he was a valuable member of the force, but it gnawed at him that he wasn't out there on the street, going right up against the bad guys. A dispatcher never got closer to the action than the telephone.

He didn't talk about it, but sometimes when he was down in the basement working out, Mom would tell us how he'd come in from work or class scowling, barely grunting a greeting as he slammed the door. He'd grab a couple beers out of the refrigerator before heading down to the basement, and that was the last anybody would see of him for the night.

IT WAS ALMOST TEN THIRTY one night when the phone rang. I was trying to get Timmy down, so I let Bob get it. Next thing I knew, he was pounding up the stairs, yelling that it was my dad. I traded the baby for the phone and said, "Dad? What's going on?" Ten seconds later, I was yanking on sweatpants while Bob grabbed the diaper bag, and ten seconds after that, we were out the door.

Every light was on at my parents' house. Police cars were in the driveway and in front of the house, lights still flashing. Neighbors stood in shivering clusters on the sidewalk, but we pushed through. At the door, Bob told the cop who we were, and he let us in.

My mother was sitting in her rocking chair. Michelle was trying to get her to take a cup of tea. Mich's eyes were teary as she insisted, "You need to drink this," but Mom kept shaking her head.

"Let me try," I said. Being the eldest has its perks, and one is the inalienable right to take over. I knelt beside Mom's chair and rested my hand on her arm. "It's okay now," I told her even though I had no idea if it was true. "You're safe now. Dad's here, and Kevin's here, and Mich and me and Bob. We're all here for you. The police are going to take care of everything, and they're going to find that guy and put him away. I promise." Michelle shot me an annoyed look, but I ignored her. It didn't matter whether I was lying. All that mattered right now was that my mother could somehow feel safe in her own home.

Behind me, I could hear Bob asking Dad, "Did he hurt her?"

I turned in time to see my father shaking his head. "Thank God, no. When she heard him, she thought it was Kevin or me coming in, and she came downstairs. She saw the guy and screamed so loud she must have scared him, because he took off. She kept screaming, and Mrs. Pellow heard her and sent Davey over." Dave Pellow, who was six foot three and nearly three hundred pounds, hadn't been called "Davey" since he was ten years old except by his parents and mine. Dad continued, "Davey called 911, and then he called Kevin's cell. I gotta get one of those." A cell phone, he meant. Neither of my parents had one. *Nobody needs me that badly*, Mom always said when the subject came up.

Reassured, I turned back to my mother. She was huddled in her chair, her face pale and stony. "You're okay," I said, smoothing her hair. "It's okay now."

Months passed before my mother was willing to be alone in the house. Luckily, Michelle was home from college for the summer, and Angie and Paul lived just a couple blocks away, so they covered most of the time when Dad and Kevin were at work. I set up the portable crib in Angie's and my old room, and I brought the baby over and stayed with Mom when I could. It wasn't easy, but we managed.

The police never caught the guy who broke into my parents' house. Mom was so shaken that all she could tell them was that he was tall and skinny with a gray hooded sweatshirt and a big garbage bag. She said his skin was light brown, but she didn't know if that meant he was light-skinned African American or Hispanic or Indian or Middle Eastern. She couldn't even guess at his age except to say he was younger than she was. Since she was almost sixty back then, that didn't narrow things down very much.

IT WAS ALMOST A year after the break-in when the phone rang Saturday night, just before midnight. By that time, life had settled down. The twins had been born a couple months earlier, and between them and two-year-old Timmy, I had my hands full. Dad had retired, and he was driving Mom nuts, but in a good way. Angie and Paul were trying to get pregnant, and Mich was applying to grad school. Since Kevin was still living at home, we didn't have to worry as much about Mom and Dad, and we all thought this was a good thing.

And then the phone rang.

Bob answered it; I was changing Shannon and clenching my teeth against the hope that some idiot butt-dialing a wrong number wouldn't waken Tristan or Timmy. A few minutes later, Bob appeared in the doorway to the nursery. One look at his face—shocked, somber, braced—and my stomach lurched.

"Who?" The word was more breath than sound.

"Everybody's okay," he said.

Relief washed over me as I plopped down in the rocker. "Then what?"

"Kevin's been arrested."

"What? What for?" The first thought in my mind was a bar brawl. There'd been a few of these over the years. Even after all this time as a dispatcher, Kevin was still touchy about not being a "real cop." I could easily picture him taking a swing at an off-duty officer who was ribbing him.

Bob shook his head. "Somebody broke into your folks' house— and Kevin shot him."

"*WHAT*?" The shriek was out of my mouth before I could think about the babies. An instant later, Tristan started whimpering, and Shannon followed him with a full-throated wail. Across the room from their cribs, Timmy sat up in his, eyes wide, and let loose with a wail of his own. Tristan caught up fast, and I switched automatically into mommy mode as two parents tried to comfort three screaming children.

"Where is he?" I shouted over the crying.

"Police station," Bob yelled back.

"Is he okay?"

"Yeah."

It was a minor relief, but right then, I'd take what I could get. Half an hour later, when the kids had settled down to a manageable level, Bob told me to go. He offered to call his mother to babysit so he could come along, but I told him not to bother. It was probably a lot of confusion over nothing, I insisted. Neither of us believed me.

The police station would have been dreary enough under normal circumstances, but in the middle of the night, it was dismal enough to make your skin crawl. The lighting was inadequate, blue-tinged fluorescent; the walls were dirty institutional cream, the floor gray linoleum. The old wooden benches where my family perched were unpadded and scratched. When I walked in, Mom and Mich were sobbing into tissues, and Angie had her hand on Dad's shoulder as he stood like a stone by a doorway. Paul was the only one who noticed my arrival.

"Izzie. You okay?" He was a big bear of a man. When he hugged me, I felt safe.

"What happened? I don't know anything. Bob just said—" I couldn't make myself repeat it.

Paul drew me off to one side. "As far as I know, some kids broke into the house, Kevin tried to stop them, and he ended up shooting one of them."

"Is Kevin okay?"

"He's okay."

"What about the kid?"

Paul hesitated. "He didn't make it."

"He's *dead*?" My baby brother had *killed* somebody? No. It wasn't possible.

"On your parents' front lawn. The kid was running away. Kevin hit him three times. Kid was dead at the scene." He rattled the details off fast, like he wanted to get away from them.

"What?" I didn't have the stomach to hear it again, but I couldn't believe I'd heard right.

"Nobody's said much yet. There were two kids. The other one's in custody. No idea what he's going to say."

"I didn't even know Kevin had a gun." Not that I should have been surprised. Granted, dispatchers didn't carry weapons, but still, there was no reason he shouldn't have one. I hadn't been down to his basement apartment in ages. For all I knew, he had an entire arsenal. "What time did this all happen?"

"About three hours ago, maybe." The round black-and-white clock on the wall proclaimed that it was now 2:17. Paul added, "Your dad called us, and that's why I called you."

"Thanks." I hadn't even thought to ask Bob who'd called. All at once, I was shivering with cold.

Running away.

Three times.

Dead at the scene.

My mother and sisters were crying. My father was ashen. My brother-in-law looked stricken. My husband was at home trying to care for three babies. My brother was in a cell somewhere. And I was standing in the lobby of the police station, begging God to figure out a way to keep Kevin from being charged with murder.

"HE WAS *PROTECTING* US!" Dad insisted the next morning as he stomped around the kitchen while Angie and I made a breakfast nobody ate. "Those sleazebags broke into *our* house! Kevin was defending *us*! Those scumbags deserved whatever Kevin did! A man is entitled to defend his home and his family! What if Kevin hadn't been home? What if it was your mother who heard them and went to see what was happening? What if they had a weapon?" The *what ifs* went on and on, punctuated by refrains of "He was defending us!"

Dad, Paul, and I were at the police station by nine o'clock Sunday morning. Mom wanted to come, but she and Mich were still crying at the slightest provocation, so Angie stayed with them at the house. Dad was irate, but at least he wasn't hysterical.

When we finally got through all the security checks, Kevin was waiting in a windowless room with no furniture except a metal table and chairs, all bolted down. He looked grim and resolute. A smattering of ginger whiskers decorated his chin. The wrinkled too-bright orange jumpsuit seemed inappropriately cheerful.

"Kev, what happened?" I asked when the guard went outside.

My brother said nothing. He was staring at the iron ring in the middle of the table. The shackles on his hands were connected by a chain the guard had fastened to that ring. He couldn't even rub his nose unless he bent down to the tabletop.

"Kevin." Paul's voice was deep. "You need to tell us what happened."

"I can't," said Kevin. "My lawyer said not to say anything."

"Lawyer? What lawyer?" The rest of us stared at one another.

"Henry P. R. Murdoch. He was here earlier this morning. Said he wants to take my case for free because it's so important. It's a landmark case about freedom." His voice was dull as he parroted the lawyer's words.

It turned out that Henry P. R. Murdoch had represented other members of the department for various indiscretions, professional and otherwise. Murdoch was especially popular among those who'd been arrested for gun-related crimes. As he proclaimed in his commercials, he was a fierce defender of the Second Amendment and a card-carrying member of the NRA. One of the pictures on his website showed him shaking hands with Charlton Heston.

"It's unfortunate our state doesn't have a 'Stand Your Ground' law," Murdoch mused when we sat down with him at home that evening.

"What's that?" I asked.

"It says you don't have to run away from a fight," he said.

"But—" I broke off.

"But what?" Mom asked.

I regretted speaking in front of her, but it was too late now. "Kevin wasn't the one running away. Ricardo Gomez was. Kevin ran after him. That's not the same thing."

"Since we don't have that law in this state, it doesn't matter," said Murdoch smoothly. "We'll just use what we have."

"And what's that?" Dad asked.

Murdoch smiled, a toothy smile that made my skin creep. "Kevin," he said. "I couldn't ask for a better defendant. He's a cop. Passionate about justice, law enforcement, protecting his family. Spotless record. This is a landmark case."

It might have been a landmark case, but that didn't get my brother out of jail. As Murdoch explained after the arraignment, a white guy had shot a Hispanic kid in the back three times, and with all the riots and protests about interracial shootings over the past few years, there was no way the non-white community was going to sit still for having that white guy parading around the streets like a hero. Plus, he wasn't just charged with shooting Gomez, as bad as that would be— the prosecutor was calling it a hate crime since Kevin had shot the Hispanic kid, but not the white one.

The protests didn't help, either. They'd started by sunrise after Gomez's death, and they grew louder and more passionate by the hour. The protestors couldn't come on my parents' property, but the sidewalk in front of the house was fair game, and there they marched back and forth, chanting and waving signs. Mourners piled candles, flowers, pictures, and stuffed animals around the telephone pole a mere sidewalk's width from the grass still stained with Gomez's blood. Between the media and the protests calling for justice for "Ricky," the noise filtering through the windows was so loud we could hardly hear each other speak.

Monday morning, we needed four cops and Davey Pellow's imposing bulk to get us out of the house and into the cars to go to the arraignment. Blue uniforms filled the courtroom as Kevin's coworkers stood in solidarity with him. The mob outside screeched about hate crimes and racial intolerance. Television cameras and well-coiffed reporters with microphones crowded the courthouse steps. The prosecutor claimed Kevin was a flight risk even though he'd lived his entire life in the same house, and Murdoch argued that Kevin was being demonized by the media. All he'd done was defend his family and his home, Murdoch insisted.

It was too big a spectacle for the judge. He denied bail, and Kevin was in for the duration.

The case made it to trial in seven months, which, according to Murdoch, was pretty good. It didn't seem good to me. My brother had been sitting in a cell all through spring and summer, and now we were midway through fall. We'd be lucky to have him home for Thanksgiving. As the thought crossed my mind, I realized I was assuming Kevin would be acquitted. Of course, he would. My little brother was a defender. Not a murderer.

Kevin had held fast to Murdoch's advice, so no one heard his side of what happened that night, but once Marcel Luciano worked out his deal and started yapping, even a blind man could see things didn't look good for Kevin. According to Luciano, Kevin yelled at them to get down on the floor, but he was waving the gun around and said he'd blow their fucking brains out if they moved. Luciano threw himself facedown on the living room rug, but Gomez made a run for it. Kevin went after him, still yelling for Gomez to stop. Luciano never moved off the rug until the police came, but he heard the gunshots. Only three, he said, and he was unshakeable in his testimony. Not that it mattered, because ballistics came up with the same answer, which was not good. Three shots and three hits, with a running target and only a streetlight for illumination. The prosecutor argued that this meant the hits were no accident, that Kevin had shot to kill rather than merely warn or wound. The other downside of the ballistics evidence, according to Murdoch, was with ballistics confirming this piece of Luciano's testimony, the jury was more likely to believe Luciano on other things as well.

"But everybody agrees what happened," I protested. "It's just a question of whether Kevin could legally do it, right? Whether he had the right to protect his home and his family—isn't that it?"

"Yes and no," said Murdoch. "Juries want to assign blame. In this case, we need for them to blame Ricardo Gomez, first for breaking into your parents' house, and then for threatening Kevin and not doing what Kevin said. The prosecutor wants the jury to blame Kevin, not just because he was the one with the gun, but because he could have let Gomez run away and instead, he killed him." My mother made a tiny whimpering sound, and Angie laid her hand on Mom's.

He killed him. It sounded so harsh, so inexcusable. According to the hospital records—Murdoch let us see them—Gomez was shot three times in the back, and any one of those bullets would have killed him. When the physician assistant from the ER was called to the stand by the prosecution, he said, "I've seen a lot of gunshot wounds in my time. If the victim was running away and the shooter still managed to plant all three bullets—well, all I can say is this guy knew what he was doing." His admiration sent chills through me.

Pow. Pow. Pow.

Got the bad guy.

The prosecution called as a witness the tall, skinny guy with bad skin who ran the police firing range. The guy said Kevin was a regular, coming in three or four times a week to practice—not that he needed much practice, because he was a terrific marksman. Gifted, in fact. Besides, he'd been taking courses for years. When I heard that, I glanced at Angie, who looked as surprised as I felt. On her other side, Mich leaned forward to catch my eye, brows drawn together in question. I shook my head slightly. No, none of us had known.

"Do you think Mom and Dad knew?" Angie asked at the recess.

"Probably not," I said. Ours wasn't a family with secrets, or so I'd always believed. Surely if my parents knew about Kevin's gun activities, it would have come up in conversation at some point.

But Kevin had never mentioned it.

"Why would he keep it a secret?" Michelle asked. "It's not like he was doing anything wrong. So, he decided he wanted to learn to shoot—so what? He's a cop. Don't they all do that?"

So what, indeed, I thought as the knock on the door behind the bench signaled that the judge was about to return. It wasn't the gun training that bothered me. It was the secrecy. It wasn't like we had any pacifists or gun control nuts in our family who would give him a hard time. Besides, if Kevin had been able to fulfill his dream of becoming a cop on the street, of course he'd have had a gun. Several, probably, and nobody would have said a thing about it, other than maybe making sure they were locked up when the kids came over to my parents' house.

That night, I went down to Kevin's apartment in the basement of my parents' home. The trunk Kevin had used as a gun case stood open and empty. When the police got a warrant to search the house, they found four guns in addition to the one Kevin used, two rifles and two handguns. The guns were all properly registered, and Kevin's orderly files contained all the correct paperwork. Nothing out of order.

A thought struck me. I rummaged through his drawer, yanked out the folders, and flipped through the pages, scanning them for dates of purchase. They'd all been purchased within a six-week period about a year and a half earlier. Something about the dates looked familiar. It took me a minute, but then, the pieces fell into place.

He'd bought all five weapons following the first break-in.

As my mother made dinner upstairs and my sisters played with the babies, I sat in Kevin's chilly basement apartment. For the first time, I understood why he still lived there. It wasn't money or convenience. He was my parents' self-appointed protector. That was his job. He might not be a cop on the street, but he was a cop here, where it counted.

"That went well," Murdoch commented during the lunch recess. He'd called Deb Satter, the middle-aged woman who owned the gun shop where Kevin had bought his weapons. Deb was plump with threads of silver in her dark hair, and she looked like somebody you might find reading to kids at the library's story hour. Murdoch continued, "Having a gun doesn't make a person a criminal. The jury needs to hear that. There's been so much garbage in the news about wacko vigilante types shooting innocent people. We need to get that image out of their heads. We need to make sure they recognize that Kevin is a normal, law-abiding citizen who responded to the break-in the way any normal, law-abiding citizen would—especially if that person's elderly parents were in the house."

"We're not 'elderly,'" Dad snapped.

Murdoch held up his hand. "My apologies," he said. "We've got some young people on the jury who think anybody over thirty-five is elderly. I'm warming up for them."

"But here's what I don't get." I was hesitant to say it out loud, but I needed to know. "I get how it's self-defense if somebody's breaking in or coming at you or something like that—but this kid was running away. How is it self-defense if you're just keeping the thief from escaping?"

Murdoch glared at me. "That's going to be a legal argument," he said after a minute, and he turned the conversation to his observations about the jurors.

At the end of the evidence, when Murdoch announced that the defense rested, the prosecutor jumped up as if he'd been waiting for that moment all week. "At this time, the prosecution wishes to make a motion outside the presence of the jury," he said. The judge didn't look surprised. He told the jury there was going to be a legal argument and they were to wait in the jury room until the clerk brought them back out.

The way the judge said it, you'd have thought there would be some dry talk with lots of case names and laws being cited. Instead, the prosecutor argued exactly what I'd feared, namely, that it wasn't self-defense because Ricardo Gomez had been running away when he was shot in the back. I couldn't follow Murdoch's argument—he used terms like "continuing course of conduct" and "reasonable force," but it didn't sound to me as if he was answering the main argument. Whatever he said, though, it was enough for the judge, who finally said, "Motion denied. Bring the jury back in."

The judge read instructions to the jury for the better part of two hours. I had no idea how they were supposed to remember what they heard. Murdoch told me later that the judge sends a copy of the instructions into the jury room along with the exhibits when deliberations begin. Even so, I couldn't imagine this group of normal-looking people—not a lawyer, cop, or professor in the bunch—figuring out what all that legal mumbo jumbo meant, much less how to apply it to the evidence.

Not that it mattered. All they needed to do was find Kevin innocent.

"Actually, it's 'not guilty,'" Murdoch said as we waited. "The finding is that the state failed to prove his guilt or that he had a legally sufficient defense." He looked quite satisfied, as if the verdict was a foregone conclusion and we were silly to be so worried.

Kevin didn't get to stay with us while the jury deliberated. Even though he had been permitted to shed the orange jumpsuit in favor of his dark gray suit and Dad's most somber tie, he was still a prisoner in the eyes of the state. The marshal took him back into lockup as soon as the jury retired.

"Don't worry," Dad called as Kevin was led away. "It'll all be fine." His tone was firm, but his eyes betrayed his anxiety, cutting back and forth from Murdoch to the rest of us.

The jury didn't reach its verdict until nearly four o'clock the next day. By that time, we were barely speaking to one another, all locked in our own little worlds. I clutched Bob's hand. Mom and Michelle cried on each other. Dad and Paul stood by the window. Angie flipped through the law books on the shelves at the front of the courtroom as if she were going to find the key to the case.

A knock from the jury room echoed through the courtroom. As one, we froze. The young clerk in the blue suit opened the door slightly. We couldn't see who was on the other side, but after only a few seconds, the clerk closed the door.

"Well?" Murdoch was on his feet.

The clerk nodded. "They have a verdict."

THE NEXT FIFTEEN MINUTES crawl by. The clerk leaves the courtroom. The prosecutor comes back in. The marshal brings Kevin in. Murdoch meets his eyes, but neither of them gives anything away.

A knock from the other side of the door behind the bench. The marshal intones, "All rise." The judge comes back out and tells us to be seated. He instructs the young clerk to bring in the jury. When they are seated, the judge asks, "Has the jury reached a verdict?"

A tall man with blond-gray hair stands. "We have." He hands a folded piece of paper to the clerk, who takes it to the judge. The judge unfolds it, reads and refolds it, handing it back without showing any reaction. The clerk takes the paper back to the tall man, and the judge asks, "What say you?"

The tall man's voice is firm and clear, but I can barely understand his words. It's as though he's speaking underwater. I hear gasps from behind me, and murmurs. Voices get louder, more agitated. The judge bangs the gavel, demanding order. My mother's hands are pressed against her mouth. Her eyes glisten. All around me, my family is trying to maintain decorum. Nobody wants to be thrown out before the judge says the magic words.

Finally, after the jury is polled and thanked and released, we hear what we've been waiting for all these months: "The defendant is hereby ordered to be released from custody. Mr. McCormick, you're free to go."

With that, the room erupts. Marshals spring into action, keeping the two sides separate. Across the aisle, Ricardo Gomez's mother wails as the prosecutor tries to say something to her. His girlfriend shrieks and sobs. His brothers scream curses at Kevin, at all of us.

Kevin doesn't seem to notice them. He barely has time to turn around before Dad engulfs him in a bear hug. Our tears spill over, except ours are tears of relief, of joy.

As Mom hugs him, Kevin looks up, over her head, at me. Our eyes meet. At first, I don't understand what I see there. Before I can reach him, the corners of his mouth quirk, and he nods ever so slightly.

Time tumbles backward. The courtroom blurs. In the midst of the chaos, I see the freckle-faced little boy who toddled triumphantly around the living room with his cap pistol. The same expression lights his eyes now as it did then.

The glint of satisfaction.

The world tilts. My heart pounds. Hot tears prick my eyes. I open my mouth, but no sound issues. Luckily, everyone is so excited that they don't notice as I sit, dizzy and cold among the jubilation. In that one instant, Kevin has torn away the merciful veil of oblivion. Gone forever are the days when I rested so easily—so naively—in blessed ignorance of who my brother really is. Who we raised him to be.

Pow. Pow. Pow.

Got the bad guy.

Della Finds Her Gift

Sandy Lender

HER BREATHING SHALLOW FROM THE LABOR OF STAYING ALIVE, HER THROAT dry from crushed dust off the mountains towering to either side of her, Della rasped, "I have nothing left." She lowered to her belly, unable to feel the rocks' edges or the hilt of the dagger kneading her waist. All senses were muted at this point.

Well, all of *her* senses were muted. From the mouth of his cave thousands of feet above, Wisgleaw heard her dying declaration clearly.

He had watched her crumble to her knees that morning; had watched her crawl toward an overhang for shelter from both of Onweald's blistering suns. To any other creature that high up the mountain, the speck of human in the crevices below would have blended into the sand like a pebble of uneven movement. To an ancient dragon whose golden eyes saw more clearly than raptors', even the scraps of Della's dress appeared ragged to him. The stink of her sweat mingled with infrequent puddles of urine and a blacksmith's bloodline trickling from scrapes on exposed limbs. It made a rank bouquet of human odor for Wisgleaw and his companion, Storm, to endure the past few days.

Storm hissed in the common language, "The human is ready to take."

"Perhaps."

Storm growled at him. "You've waited too long to get answers without a fight. This one's dead. And if you wait any longer to collect the body, the edras will get there first."

Wisgleaw considered that. The human below had made no effort to cover her tracks. The only reason edras hadn't taken her yet was her good fortune to stumble into Wisgleaw's territory.

Well, good fortune for him.

"I'll collect her before she dies," Wisgleaw said.

"The council won't like it. No human's walked into these mountains for a decade and you want to talk to it before you eat it. What if others come looking for it? We'll be exposed because you want that sword."

Wisgleaw spun on his companion, ferocious and terrifying. His jaws snapped within a foot of her snout, and the power of his bite sent a concussive force through the cave. It punched Storm in the face, knocking loose three red scales that clattered to the rock floor. "I will do as I please," he roared.

Hot breath blasted Storm's face. She winced, blinking her eyes against pain, as the vapor blistered the skin under the softer scales on her neck.

"You will not speak of it to any dragon," he commanded.

Storm would've bowed her head if not for painful welts rising under her scales. "As you wish."

She turned in the wide space, her reddish-brown tail snaking to follow her body's curve, and she lumbered into the depths of the mountain to hide. Wisgleaw roared from the maw of his cave to establish his claim on the easy meal and watched dark shapes slink back into the shadows. The demons and mountain cats left the prey to the alpha predator. He launched himself toward the chasm, measuring the distance with a dragon's perfection to swoop, glide, and land with as little disruption as the wild eagles along the shores of the Meredore. Graceful. Precise. Easily dismissed.

His foreclaws could manipulate objects gently, and he picked up the human, turning her carefully. Cradling her upper torso in the width of his claw, he could rest her head against one talon to stare at her features. This youngling, coated with dust from the Anthelk Mountains, had tracks and smudges of muddy tears around her eyes and under her nose. Cracks in the mud proved she'd run out of moisture. She was dehydrated. He'd get no answers from her if he let her die.

Thus began a month-long process of watering and washing the human in a pool in his cave. He began by removing her dagger, which couldn't kill him, of course, but could inflict a painful scratch. He mashed berries from branches of trees on the east side of the mountains, nearest the Valley of Fayshafte, to then press into her mouth to restore her. He placed a dress from his treasure horde near her so she could wear the cleaner, better-repaired garment if she regained the energy to change into it. Within a week, she had gathered enough strength to sit up and stare at him in abject terror, so he introduced himself.

Della gulped back fear and asked the first thing that came to mind. "How do you speak the common language?"

"This is your question? I've saved your life and you want to know how I can talk to you?"

"I have others," she said. She didn't want to waste her questions if the creature imposed a limit. As if denying her nervousness, she swallowed what could have been a sob and blurted out, "How do you exist? Dragons are gone. The last year anyone saw a dragon was before the year 6500 of records. The priests say dragons are extinct. This can't be real in—"

"You sound upset," he interrupted.

"Yes, I'm upset." She coughed. Her throat still hurt from the days of dehydration, and her chest crackled with the effort of breathing thin air. "You're a dragon!"

"You're a human, yet you don't see me upset about your presence here."

Della tilted her head slightly, causing a chunk of her greasy black hair to shift over her shoulder. His statement had puzzled her, and, apparently, he understood enough about human expressions to realize it.

"You humans are dangerous creatures with your stabbing of spears and firing of arrows," he explained with a gravelly, calm voice. "As you said, dragons are supposed to be extinct. That's because humans set out to hunt us all down. Even wars with each other don't stop humans from sneaking into our lairs to kill us in our sleep.

"When you walked past the fen to the foothills of the mountains, I watched for more to follow you. I expected a hunting party. I expected you to brandish some kind of bow and arrow. Instead, you wandered around until you were close to death, leaving a trail any mountain kitten could follow. What's wrong with you? And why haven't more come looking for you?"

Della saw no reason for subterfuge. Wisgleaw would either kill and eat her or he'd not. She remained seated with her bones pressed against the cave wall because she lacked the strength to move, but she looked away from the brackish-colored reptile. Instead, she stared at the cool cerulean of the pool where he'd cared for her. She watched its rippling surface, massaged by the soft trickle of water from a crevice in the stones, lit by a shaft of dusty sunlight from a crevice in the ceiling. The peacefulness of the pool offered a contrast to the menacing teeth and talons of a dragon towering a few feet in front of her.

He had a point. He'd saved her life and tended to her despite her humanity. He must have a use for her besides eating. She could tell him that she'd made herself utterly alone in Onweald, and even if she *shouldn't* trust him with that information, what did it matter?

"I left my father's home at night. No one knew I was leaving or where I was going. If anyone followed me, they wouldn't have followed all the way across the fen."

"I can't believe humans would allow a female to come to harm."

She huffed a cynical sort of laugh, fingering the simple garment he'd placed near her. It would hang on her starving frame. "You know a lot about the human world beyond our language, don't you?"

"Tell me how a female got away from her family," he pressed.

"My father hasn't promised me to anyone yet. He says no one in our village can offer a high enough price. There's another girl in our village who'll fetch a decent price for her family, if one of my brothers doesn't beat them to it. My father is a blacksmith. I assume you know what that is?"

"I do."

She didn't realize he growled the answer, and she continued. "Of course, you do. My father made a great deal of coin during the sand wars, which is how he was able to pay a dowry for a wife. This means he can bide his time and command any price he wants for me. He's waiting for a wealthy merchant to come through Kharole."

"So, you *are* from the village of Kharole? North of the fen?"

"I am."

"The village of the sword," he breathed.

The heat of his breath reached her as he finished the words, and she wondered why a dragon cared about a sword. She wondered how he knew the priests had a cursed weapon in the village. She turned her head to fix him in her dark gaze. "We have a sword in the temple," she confirmed.

"The sword no human can hold for a full battle."

She frowned. "How do you know that?"

"I'm an old dragon whose scales grow brittle. I'll sire no more eggs."

"That means you know about pretty swords?"

"You have a saucy tongue," he said. "Does your father let you speak that way to him?"

She almost smiled. Almost. The ancient dragon saw the hint of amusement cross her face, saw the glimmer of shine in her midnight-blue eyes, but it passed like shadow.

"He requires respect as any parent would. I didn't leave home because of my father or because I someday have to breed children for our world. I left because we're all starving.

"I watched my brother Frederick die of sickness that couldn't be cured because he was too weak from hunger, too weakened by lack of food. I left because it's stupid to wait for a wealthy man to come through and pay a sack of coin that buys nothing. There's nothing to buy. The dagger I assume you've taken from me could have bought a loaf of bread if there was a loaf of bread to buy. But the land that surrounds Kharole has seen too many years of failed crops. The cotton produces weak cloth."

She held out her arms with the tatters of her sleeves hanging to prove that point, and then dropped them again.

"The people are afraid to try anything to improve their chances for good crops next year. I left—" This time there was no mistaking she gulped back a sob. "I left because I couldn't watch anyone else starve to death while we waited for help."

Wisgleaw tapped one talon on the cave floor as he considered her words. "Where were you going to sell your dagger?"

She shook her head. "I don't know. I don't think I planned to live this long."

"You planned to leave your family to fend for themselves."

"Don't judge me." She put no energy behind the request. "You don't know how it is there. People are dying slow, painful deaths."

"I'm not judging you. I merely state the fact: You left your family with no hope, didn't you?"

His callous words brought her to tears, and he took that as a good sign. After a moment of watching her try to calm her emotions, he said, "I apologize. Perhaps you believed your family had no hope even before you left?"

She nodded, still crying, still dabbing her red and puffy eyes with a strip of her sleeve.

"Tell me your name," he suggested.

"Della Smithieson."

Of course, her name echoed the typical female naming convention of Onweald. To find favor with the gods, parents named their daughters after the lesser goddess Ella Jentol. In this case, it wasn't working. Yet.

"Della Smithieson, I think you should rest."

She sniffled, wiping her nose with her sleeve. "I think so, too."

"I have more questions for you, but they can wait for another day. When you're stronger. When you feel more at ease."

"More at ease," she huffed. "With a giant dragon I was told didn't exist."

He chuckled at her. "Giant. No, Della. I'm not one of the giant dragons. But I appreciate your flattery."

ANOTHER WEEK OF MASHED berries and fish gave Della more strength. She could crawl to the edge of the pool to give herself water and could crawl to a hole near a wall of the cave to void her bladder or bowels. She attempted to brush her hair with her fingers and found it a mass of tangles. She gave up, not caring what her hair looked like when a dragon decided to eat her. One day, he gave her a jeweled comb from his treasure horde before dropping a fish onto a wood plank before her and grumbling something about rain being scarce.

"As it has been for many seasons," she agreed. She took a flat rock to scale the fish while he watched from a few feet away.

"You say *many seasons*. How many have you seen?"

"Are you mocking me or asking how old I am? I'm sixteen years old."

"Is that old enough to know stories from the sand wars?"

"Some stories. My father made spear and arrow tips for the wars."

When Wisgleaw didn't respond to that, she looked up at his face to see he had closed his eyes. She didn't realize he fought the urge to set the cave interior on fire, consuming both of them and boiling the pool to vapor. When he opened his eyes, the golden irises had turned a deep orange like her father's forge.

"Tell me what you think your people of Kharole should try to improve the crops for next season."

She tilted her head slightly, taken aback by the abrupt change of subject. She wasn't offended that the dragon didn't want to talk about her family's trade; she'd rather not think about the starving family she'd left behind. Talking about how to help them was a kinder conversation.

"I think they should burn the fields now, before winter sets in, then turn the ash under to rejuvenate the soil."

His eyes popped open wider. "Where did a young female learn such a thing?"

She didn't smile at the condescending question, but a flush of pleasure swept through her veins. "I learned it from my mother. Well, I should say, I learned it from her drawings. My mother passed when I was born, may Dezurine carry her swiftly to Paradise, so I had papers with drawings she'd done. There's even one that had been the wrapping of one of Father's drifts that he'd shipped over from Bellan, and it shows how the tool can be used in turning the soil. I think my mother was wise. She understood much of farming. Her father was a grain merchant, which is why he was able to afford a wife and have children.

"But I left those papers with my father and brothers. I didn't think they were mine to take."

Wisgleaw nodded his large head, his snout bobbing lightly up and down. She assumed this was to encourage her to proceed, not merely to acknowledge the death of the family's matriarch.

"My mother's drawings showed one season to grow corn, then to burn the fields with the stalks, then to turn the ashes under the dirt, then to grow wheat the next season, then to burn the chaff, then to turn the ashes under the dirt, then to grow corn the next season, and so on. I've never seen any of the farmers burn any of the fields for as long as I've been alive. And the cotton they grow in the fields closest to the fen has gotten mold in it. It can't be used for anything anymore. It can't be sold. It would be wise to turn it into ash."

"Did you share your mother's drawings with any of the farmers?"

"Of course. But I'm just a girl. No man who's been farming all his life would listen to a girl interpreting the drawings of a woman, especially when it contradicts what he knows."

Wisgleaw puffed a breath of hot air to show his disdain. "Humans are sorry creatures. You could have saved your village with this knowledge." He thought about this for a moment, watching her scale the fish. "You may save your village yet."

Without looking back at him, she asked quietly, "Why should *you* care if I help a village full of humans who once wished to hunt your kind to extinction?"

"Because I wish to have the sword that no one human can hold. If I help you save your village, will you bring the sword to me?"

Della stared at him as if to gauge his sincerity. "Well, yes, I suppose, yes. But are you going to set the fields on fire? How does that save Kharole? I'm just one person after that. How do I return there and convince them to do anything except go dragon hunting again? You realize they'll come after you if you set their fields on fire? They believe dragons are extinct. You want them to keep believing that, right?"

It occurred to her that she shouldn't care whether or not the people of Kharole knew Wisgleaw was involved in their salvation—should she? His kindness toward her required payment in the form of her silence. This was a given. But why did she fear for his safety?

"Yes, I want them to believe dragons are gone from this world," he said. "But we can hide the fact that a dragon has burned their fields. You can return from this journey to your people with knowledge, with wisdom, with practices from a fertile land."

"You could be a bard telling stories in the village square."

"We dragons have a propensity for poetry and riddles. I can help you prepare the story you tell."

That idea pleased her, but her mind still thought ahead. "Can you help me find seeds?"

"Ah, yes, for planting in the spring. We can gather seeds out of the valley. Are you afraid of flying?"

"I haven't tried it," she said.

"You're being saucy again."

"It was a saucy question to ask a human."

"Fair enough. When you're stronger, I can carry you to the valley and you can gather seeds. It's almost time for that."

"I better get stronger soon," she said. "I can feel a chill in the air."

"Everything will go to seed before the next moon cycle," he predicted. "I'll look among my treasure for something you can use as a bag. You had nothing with you when you came into the foothills. No bag, no water horn, nothing."

"Ah, I'd lost some things in the fen. And then a dragon took my dagger."

He snorted. "I'll give your dagger back to you. I haven't flown over the fen in years," he mused. "I've had no reason to. But I have other items that humans before you have carried into these mountains. Items you may need."

Della lifted her hand in gesture toward the water. "I suppose they came here to drink from the pool and left trinkets in payment?"

"Yes, but I ate them for teasing me with their saucy tongues."

Wisgleaw noticed that she lowered her hand in a controlled manner, not in the floppy, exhausted manner with which she had been moving the past two weeks. It was a sign of improvement.

Over the next week, Wisgleaw brought her fish from a deeper area of cleaner water in the fen and discussed the swamp's decline in edible greenery. He didn't have an explanation, but he agreed with her that something was wrong in the fen south of Kharole, something that fed into the cotton fields and ruined the crop.

"Do you want to burn it, too?" he asked one day.

She grinned at him through a bite of fish. "A wet swamp? That might be difficult to explain. Remember we're supposed to be hiding the *dragon* in this strategy."

"There is that." He chuckled in his gravelly voice. "Are any of the people in your village familiar with the geasa?"

Della choked on air and started to cough. "You cannot be serious."

"I am. If you convince the people you have the geasa, you can convince them that *you* start the fire that consumes the fields and swamp. You'll be hailed—"

"I don't think you understand how people view the geasa."

"How people view it?" he asked.

"They're likely to start a fire that consumes *me*."

"I don't understand that," the dragon groused. "They build palaces where the geasa'n train."

"Where have you heard that?"

"I know of a conclave in Mon'dore where geasa'n are trained. It's a fortress with battlements that you couldn't give me enough gold to fly near."

"That may be the only one," Della mused. "I can tell you that most people fear the geasa and everything about it."

He blinked his golden dragon eyes at her. "That confuses me."

They stared at each other a moment.

"Greatly," he continued. "It confuses me greatly. Doesn't anyone understand the usefulness of having a geasa'n in the village? For example, one could stir the elements to fight off a dragon who came to steal a sword."

She gave him a derisive look as if to suggest his joke wasn't funny.

"It's a gift breathed into a human by the gods themselves," he continued. "This should not be feared; it should be celebrated."

Della wasn't going to argue that point. "Dragons must be more tolerant of differences among their peers than humans. In my village, if someone is different, that person is looked at with suspicion. You can't always trust someone who is from another village or, as the village elders say, someone who has the geasa. It's feared, rather than recognized as some kind of gift."

Wisgleaw barely shook his head, as if trying to understand. "It was my hope you'd tell the villagers that you have the geasa, and that is how you would explain burning the fields so precisely. Instead, you could tell them the sword is infused with the geasa. Will that encourage them to release it?"

"Release it?"

"Yes. I want you to bring the sword to me. That will be easier if the people think it's possessed of something they fear."

She nodded. "I can work with that. We already know it's cursed. I can take the sword from the temple and get everyone to believe it's a tool of the geasa. I then go out to the field at dusk and hand the sword to you; you take care of the fire and stay hidden to make sure it stays under control. Then the next morning, I can tell everyone that the geasa destroyed the sword.

"It's a lie, but I think I can justify the telling of it." She watched her hands in her lap while she spoke. "I think I can tell a lie if it's one that helps everyone, that protects them in the end. It protects you and any other dragons out there as well. Telling the truth would only end with deaths . . ."

Ignoring her moral dilemma, he said, "I will teach you how to hold the sword."

After all the things the dragon understood about humans and their world, she no longer questioned his knowledge of how to trick the mind into holding a cursed sword. And it never occurred to her to ask why Wisgleaw wanted it.

DELLA WALKED QUIETLY PAST the first mud and wattle hut on the outskirts of Kharole. The village into which she stepped had a solemnness about it—an almost silence. No village on this side of Onweald had an abundance of children thanks to the sand wars that had lasted nearly two decades and the crop failures that had followed, but the lack of children here reminded Della of ongoing famine. Ongoing sadness.

The absence of cheerful noises gave the blacksmith's work a quiet backdrop for each hammer blow. Each clang rang and banged off her ears as she made her way toward the startling strikes and the sudden hiss of hot iron in water. Her father working under the open-air wooden frame lifted steaming tongs from a barrel of water, and his eyes shifted their focus from the instruments in front of him to Della.

He let his hands fall to his sides, relaxing their grips on the hammer and tongs so that they fell, thumping and clumping to the dirt ground. His jaw slackened so that his mouth fell open.

She spoke calmly to him. "I've come home with a way to help the village."

"Della!" someone shouted. One of her brothers ran across the dusty cart path toward her, shouting her name repeatedly with excitement.

Soon, members of the village shuffled out of huts to see if it was true. Had the daughter of Frederick Smithieson the Second come back? The elders invited Frederick, Della, and the last two Smithieson sons to the temple in the village square to discuss what was going on. It took less than an hour for a majority of the village's population to assemble there.

"I ran away," Della was explaining as people filed in to listen. "I couldn't bear to watch any more of my family die after Frederick in the spring. Without me, there'd be more food for Derick and Orick. And . . . and I thought I might find help. But my reason for running away was selfish. I couldn't watch . . ."

Frederick put a grizzled hand on his daughter's shoulder. "Tell us who helped you. Whom do we owe?"

She shook her head. "I don't remember everything." This was not the lie. Yet.

"I walked through the fen, and it's poisoned. Something bad is happening there and that's what's creeping into our cotton fields. By the time I got to the foothills of the Anthelk Mountains, I was near death. I climbed into the mountains, but I got lost and disoriented. I woke up in a cave at one point. There was a pool of water I could drink from. I regained some strength there. Someone must have helped me. Someone must have brought me food. I remember eating fish."

"From the pool?" her brother Derick asked.

"Perhaps," she said.

Her father frowned at her strange response.

"But I went to the Valley of Fayshafte and I collected seeds." She pointed at the satchel she'd carried. "And I learned what we must do to make the crops grow next season." She walked to the altar and gestured to the sword that had been resting there for decades. "And I learned how this will help us."

Remembering what Wisgleaw had said, she gently but quickly rubbed her fingertips across the pads of her thumbs to trigger the subconscious response he'd taught her. Then she used both hands to pick up the sword, one hand grasping the hilt, one hand sliding carefully under the decorated blade. As she did so, as she lifted the weapon, she almost believed it *was* touched by the geasa. She heard the music of wooden flutes and harps in harmony and a soft choir of delicate voices.

Melody glided through halls of the hiding
Softly and lowly and gently and calmly
Maidens who huddled together were dreaming
Whispering wings of a dove softly bringing
Comfort of nestling in songbirds' soft singing
Something to ease them and brace them for mourning

She shook her head to clear the music from her brain and turned back to the congregation. As if time had stood still while she listened to the song in her mind, the men sat in motionless surprise.

One of them gasped. "Be careful."

"It won't burn her immediately," the priest near her said.

She spoke to Priest Ghall: "It will start to burn soon, but I'll wear leather gloves to take this to the fields outside the village gates." She held the sword over her head for dramatic flair and raised her voice as Wisgleaw had made her practice. "And it will burn the weeds and thistles and mold that have choked out our cotton and wheat. This is a tool of the geasa'n. This sword was placed here to one day save us! That day has come! We have in our midst an element, a gift from the gods!"

Gasps and mutterings answered her.

"I will wield this tool to char the useless bramble. Then we can work together as a village to turn the soil. We will prepare it for next season. The burned bramble will restore and fertilize the ground. It will kill what's rotted our cotton from below the dirt and offer nutrients to grow something good. With these seeds and renewed ground, we will have excellent crops next year. We will have a food that can make bread again, and it will be enough to feed our families and store up for winter and sell to villages to the north. We will survive!"

"You should put that down," someone reminded her.

IT TOOK MORE THAN an hour to convince the priest and others to let her carry out her task. In the end, they agreed because she had held the sword for an uncomfortably long period of time. Legend had it that men had carried the sword into battle by sharing the burden. One warrior would pass the sword to a fellow warrior who would pass it to the next and so on. In this fashion, they were able to wield the gifted blade without being burned by its power to protect the village of Kharole more than once.

She wrapped it in a burlap sack to carry it back to her father's home, and no one questioned why that worked for her. At least, no one questioned it out loud.

"Why today?" Frederick asked his daughter. "You just got back, and we should find a way to celebrate. There isn't much food, but we can . . . we can all be together."

Della frowned. "I'm not going away. I'll get the fields ready overnight and we can celebrate something special tomorrow."

"Having you back is something special," Derick said.

"Della, did anyone tell you yet the Eldersons had a daughter?" Orick asked, setting a plate of skinny root vegetables in the middle of the family's table. "There are three girls in the village now that you've returned."

"She's the cutest little thing," Derick confirmed.

"Have you started building a house for her already?" Della teased.

"Don't be silly."

"Don't give your brother a saucy tongue," Frederick said.

She finished pulling on leather gloves and popped one of the small vegetables in her mouth. That left the three larger ones for her three older family members. She picked up the roll of burlap that contained the sword. Talking around the glob in her mouth, she said, "I'll make a bit of bread out of some of those seeds. We'll need as many of them as we can save to plant after winter, but I know everyone's hungry here."

"We can grind some and add that to the dust flour," Orick said.

"I think that's a good plan," she said. "In the meantime, do you have a container that will hold some of the seeds? Something that will keep them dry?"

"You fear them being stolen," her father stated. It wasn't a question.

She nodded.

"You have so little faith in your neighbors?"

"I have little faith in people who are starving. Or whose children are starving."

"There are few children left alive," Orick murmured.

She grimaced. "There you have it. Please put half the seeds in a container that you can hide somewhere safe. Somewhere no one will think to look for it. Then set aside just a bit for us to make bread with tomorrow. If someone tries to take seeds tonight, don't give your life defending this satchel, but don't give it up too easily, either."

Frederick sat heavily at the table, staring at the plate of sparse and unappealing vegetables. "It pains me to have my children think such things. To be conniving."

"You're sure you don't want one of us going with you?" Derick asked. "I know Father would feel better if you had help."

Della gave her brother a sort of half smile. "Father would?"

"We all would."

"I love you, too, my brother. But this is something I should do on my own. I'll be back by morning, I'm sure." She believed it as she said it.

The menfolk watched her walk toward the south of the village, watched her wave at someone as she passed a leaning house. Wisgleaw also watched her leaving the village, but he watched with dragon eyes from behind a cluster of fallen trees and tall bramble alongside one of the cotton fields north of the fen. Of course, he stayed close to the fen so he could slip back into the depths of swamp and shadow if Della double-crossed him.

Somehow, she knew exactly where he hunkered behind the thistles and wood, as if she could discern the outline of dragon horns from the jagged curves of dead branches. She made her way through the fetid cotton, brushing the burs from her skirt when particularly thorny pricks grabbed hold, and walked in a crooked yet certain path to him.

As she approached, she spoke. "We have another hour at least until it's fully dark. Is it safe to begin?"

She held out the sword to him.

"I'm pleased with you, Della Smithieson. Thank you for being true to your word."

"Why wouldn't I be? We have a good plan."

"Yes, but humans are not always reliable." He slid the wrapped sword into a sheath-like pouch that he had strapped to his forearm. It bulged only slightly along the outline of a dragon's muscles under smooth, brackish-colored scales. "Just as dragons are not always dependable," he continued. "But you and I have a friendship that makes us accountable to one another."

"Are you suggesting you wouldn't have kept your word?"

"There are members of the dragon council who would prefer I set fire to the village rather than help the villagers survive and thrive."

"Those dragons must be a disappointment to you."

"Perhaps. Come along. Let's get you a safe distance from the weeds. I can control only so much of the flame. To see you harmed would make me sad."

She believed him and followed the lumbering creature whose grace in flight was much more accomplished than his movement on land. It was as they moved into the fen for better concealment that their plan began to fall apart.

Wisgleaw put his snout into the air and sniffed. He didn't growl, but he looked down at the human walking beside him. She hadn't noticed him smelling the group of villagers who had followed her; the villagers whose scent included the blacksmith's bloodline. He wondered if she knew they had tracked her. She wasn't sly of movement, wasn't difficult to track. Anyone could have followed her for any number of reasons. He would have to solve the problem.

WHEN MORNING DAWNED OVER smoky land, a mix of orange and pink light reflected off the ash and dust in the air. Both of Onweald's suns were up by the time Della could breathe properly after the heat and burning of the night before. Whatever creeping mold had come into the cotton field had let off a noxious stench as it went up in flames, sending her into an almost hallucinatory state. She had collapsed from lack of breath, from the inability to fill her lungs properly. Wisgleaw had pulled her deeper into the fen for protection and fanned the smoke away from her until she regained consciousness.

By the time she was ready to face the village again, he brought her a shallow basket from his treasure horde. It was filled with fresh fish.

"I guess this is where we say goodbye," she said. Something about saying it out loud caused a twinge in her chest. And she didn't think that was just the smoke lingering in her lungs. The bit of sadness she felt was due to parting ways with a companion who'd saved her life a mere month before.

"Perhaps," he answered. "If there should be anything else you require, you may return to my cave in the Anthelk Mountains."

"Cryptic."

The dragon huffed. "You've proved you are a human who can keep her word. If you need a home, I can hide you."

Della smiled at that and began a much easier hike back through the still smoldering cotton field of stinking ash. She carried the basket that would be much welcomed by her family. Along the way, she wondered how many people in Onweald had an open invitation to visit a dragon's cave. It gave her a sense of pride to think she would be able to go into the Anthelk Mountains and find a huge reptile friend there. Of course, she could never tell anyone such a thing.

Keeping such a secret would be lonely.

By the time she approached her father's house, she realized no one was out in the village. Again. No one awaited her return. No one stood outside their homes or the temple to ask if the burning had been successful, to ask if the sword made it through unscathed, to see if Della returned unharmed. She walked up to her father's home where she could hear a man's voice inside, tense and serious. Because she didn't recognize the priest's voice at first, she stopped outside the open window and listened.

"I don't think you understand," Priest Ghall was saying. "No one can wield a tool of the geasa unless he has traces of the geasa within him. If it's true that the sword is possessed of it, then your daughter cannot use that force unless she's tainted—"

"Enough! I won't hear it."

"But you *must* hear it. Your daughter is stained by the curse. She took the sword and burned the fields with it, just as she said she would. She killed men from our village with her lack of control. She killed her own brothers, her own flesh and blood."

At the priest's startling words, Della's heartbeat thumped

strangely in her ears. Had men from the village been so untrusting that they'd followed her into the burning fields? A mix of horror and grief stabbed her chest; it took her breath until she saw darkness caving around her. She gulped for air. She gulped for understanding.

Wisgleaw had sacrificed men who'd followed her. There was no other explanation for what Priest Ghall said about holding her accountable versus assuming her innocence through lack of control. Holding onto the wall of her father's house, she fought for consciousness, fought for comprehension.

"When Della returns, you must find a way to hide her until everyone forgets what she did," Priest Ghall recommended.

"You're not suggesting we destroy her?"

The lack of emotion in her father's voice struck Della, worsening the throbbing pain in her head.

"She's a female; our society needs her no matter what she's done. We could hide her at the temple for the rest of her life. She'd be safe there."

Frederick scoffed at that. "You're looking for a wife, are you? One you don't have to pay a dowry for?"

Della couldn't listen anymore. Her dragon companion had helped her prepare the village for survival but had labeled her dangerous and untouchable in the process. She had no home here now. Her brothers were dead, her father apathetic, her priest accusing.

She at least had the presence of mind to keep the basket before running away. She emptied most of it under the window, the splat and splelch of stiffening fish rising with their unpleasant scent. With one hand on her forehead, as if she could hold pain and confusion in one place, the other holding the basket to her hip, she stumbled away from the house. Of course, the door opened behind her. Of course, they'd heard her leaving the parting gift. "Della, wait!"

It wasn't her father who called her back. No, Frederick Smithieson the Second hid in shame and grief while Priest Ghall chased after his cursed daughter.

Della didn't stop, but she saw threadbare curtains in wattle hut windows move for spying eyes to watch how this would unfold. She continued trudging toward the north gate as she called, "Let me go on my way."

"We can help you. Stay here and let us protect you."

Turning to walk backwards yet fix him in a dark glare she didn't mean, she pulled a fish from the basket. She waved it in what she hoped looked like some menacing geasa'n pattern. "I'll weave a spell to kill you if you don't let me go on my way."

He stopped walking and spread his arms as if welcoming her back. "My dear, you can't use the geasa to harm another," the priest lied.

Della didn't laugh at him, didn't respond at all except to turn back to the north and keep walking, keep trudging with uncertain steps to the north, away from the fen, away from the Anthelk Mountains with the dragon who'd manipulated her, away from everything she used to know. Leaving Kharole a month before had set her up for a harsh education, and she wasn't sure yet if she appreciated it or not. She certainly missed her brothers and found herself weeping openly for them.

By dusk, she found a secluded glen to sit down and rest. Ripe berries and her two fish kept her fed and hydrated while she weighed her options. Words Wisgleaw had used during the past month echoed in her brain.

He'd told her the humans should revere the geasa, not fear it. But she'd get no reverence in Kharole. While it had always been expected she'd marry and have babies for their world, she'd never had to fear doing it from the confines of the temple's dark places. Alone. Reviled.

Wisgleaw had told her she could return to his cave at any time, but she couldn't trust the creature again. He'd manipulated too many elements to get the sword he coveted. She pulled the jeweled comb he'd given her from her pocket and stared at the pretty thing. She could trade it for a fine bed and meal in the right village. Considering she wore a good dress in new condition, she could probably convince a merchant that the comb was her own and not stolen. She just had to keep herself clean and healthy until then. With a heavy sigh, she looked up to the clouds gathering for nightfall and whispered, "I may not have much left, but I can work with this."

She walked again to get farther from Kharole and her old beliefs. She walked until her steps became more certain and more sure. She walked all the way to the conclave in Mon'dore, the conclave where Wisgleaw said humans built a palace to train those with traces of the geasa.

Approaching Dollywood

David Brendan Hopes

ARTHUR LIKED TO DO BORING THINGS, BUT HE WAS NOT A BORING PERSON, AND that interested me. Back where I grew up, we assumed that if it wasn't fun right off, it was not worth worrying about. Try the rutabaga once and then get on with your life. Go to the opera, hate it, never go back. Arthur was the type who'd go back ten times to see what people were raving about, then one day his face would light up and he'd get it, and become in turn one of *those* people, yapping about great tenors and divas and La Scala and what have you. He had lots of friends, of a certain kind, and I wondered why he kept after me, until the thought crossed my mind that he was maybe treating me the same way, trying to cure an initial aversion by frequent and determined contact.

Arthur was absolutely nondiscriminating when it came to information. He'd listen while the janitor told him, as though anybody had asked, how to choose the best mop for such-and-such a floor. He'd listen while my dumbass freshman roommate, Ricky or Dicky or whatever it was, went on about his dad and him were going to shoot tin cans off the fence all Thanksgiving break. I watched him listening to the waitress at the Moose Head Diner like she was Mrs. Shakespeare, and I was divided equally between the urge to mock and the urge to remake myself in his image, to empty the smarmy little vessel of my mind and let the rest of the world pour in. It was a passing fancy, but a strong one. We were in college, and surely that's what we all were supposed to be doing, asking questions, probing, inquiring. Most of my friends spent at least some of their energy trying to fend off information that was too unlike what they knew before. Not old Arthur. He could sit down in any room, amid any crowd, and come away with something learned, some new amazement about the multiplicity of the world. I wondered if he was Frankenstein's monster or somebody like, totally empty before he stepped onto campus.

Anyway, near the end of fall semester, Arthur conceived in his complicated heart the notion of going to Dollywood. Dollywood is an amusement park in Pigeon Forge, Tennessee, which started out as a bunch of other things—a coal mining theme park, a Famous Serial Killers of the Smokies theme park, I forget what all—but ended up as a kind of hillbilly heaven with country singer Dolly Parton as patron saint. I had been there, and he had not. Mom and Dad took my sisters and me there long ago, and I retained a set of intense memories—the taste of vomit in my mouth after the coaster rides, which only cotton candy could take away, for instance—which I wanted to test against my present sensual armament. Arthur didn't seem the Dollywood type, if I remembered the place correctly, but he was the try-out-new-things type. I thought I should warn him about what he was in for, but when the moment came, I realized I didn't *know* what he was in for. A ten-year-old sees one thing, a twenty-one-year-old another. Maybe he would be able to tell me what it was all about.

"Man, why do you want to go to Dollywood?"

"I've never been there. I keep hearing about it," Arthur said, lifting one blond eyebrow the way he does. You keep hearing about hell, too, but I doubt you want to go there. Still, I was game. Maybe I liked it when I was a kid. There'd been a few too many reefers between then and now for me to remember exactly.

Arthur had to drive because my tires were shot. I thought I mentioned that we should bring a buddy or two along to share the experience and the expense, but maybe I forgot, because his car was empty when he pulled up to my apartment. But then my buddies, Jo-Jo and Carnage and Alamo, began to pile in the backseat. I had to ride shotgun because I'd hurt my knee in intramural soccer and it still hurt some if I didn't have room to stretch it out from time to time.

Arthur took Jo-Jo and Carnage and Alamo in stride, and they he, once they got over his rule about no smoking in the car. Alamo can be a card when he's in the mood, and he kept Arthur laughing most of the way. I was glad that the friends I had from two different segments of my life were getting along. I was glad also that Arthur was playing some pretty cool CDs, indie rock and the like, for it's a rule that the driver owns the airwaves and if the driver likes listening to crap, you're in for hours of misery. Alamo and Arthur got into a pretty detailed discussion about the Smiths, reciting lyrics to each other in a way that I found to be, after a while, impressive. While they quoted and cross-referenced, I watched the landscape rolling by, the blue mountains in the distance, the frost-browned grass on the sides of the road stretching up to the block walls of the outlet malls. The going was slow because of the thousands of shoppers crowding to the outlets in Sevierville and Pigeon Forge, it being the week before Thanksgiving and America's Christmas acquisition panic fully upon them. Arthur asked if we wanted to stop, and maybe one of us did, but he wouldn't have said so. I figured I could pick Mom and my sisters up a few cute things in Dollywood, with the name written on it and all. They would appreciate that.

I don't think he knew what the lines of cars were after. "Look at all the traffic. Out here in the country and all. Is there a . . . I don't know. An attraction?" Arthur asked.

"All them outlets," said Carnage, waving his hand from the backseat toward the horizon.

"Outlets?"

"Yeah," Alamo continued, "where you get things cheap. You know, goods from all the big stores. They sell them cheap here."

Arthur considered this for a moment. "How cheap? What would I save if I went into that Eddie Bauer store and bought a coat?"

"You need a coat?"

"No. Just for instance."

"Couple of bucks."

"There are license plates from Florida, Alabama, Pennsylvania . . ."

"Yeah, so? My mom comes here from Atlanta every year."

"But you can't save enough to make up for gas and traveling time and all that."

Carnage was a sort of sociology major at the time, so he chimed in, "It's the swarm mentality, you know? You like to be with hundreds of other people doing the same thing they are doing because you have the idea that it must be the right thing if everybody is doing it. Christmas morning, after all the gifts are unwrapped, you can brag about the forty bucks you saved by going to the outlet stores. Nobody mentions the two hundred that went into gas and lunch and—if you're from freaking Michigan the way that lady is—motel rooms. Everybody knows it, but it's not mentioned."

Jo-Jo chimed in from the left rear window, "It's just like organized religion."

Everything nasty or questionable was like organized religion to Jo-Jo, who was a self-begotten Native American Buddhist, but I could see Arthur didn't know this was an automatic response, and he was really considering it. All he said, though, all he said from the point to the Dollywood parking lot was, "Hmmmm."

You take a tram car from the parking lot to the gates of the amusement park, and while we were waiting and riding, Arthur had time to complete his survey of his new companions. He was really pretty good at that, asking a few precise questions, showing real interest, filing it all away under the thatch of blond hair. Turned out both Alamo and Carnage were poets. They never told me. They'd told Arthur as we were stomping around against the cold, waiting for the next tram, smooth as if it had been their phone numbers. Arthur asked to read their poetry, and I bet the two of them no more than got home that night than they were emailing Arthur the hip-hop secrets of their hearts.

Jo-Jo had nothing to share poetry-wise. Jo-Jo was tactile. He felt his way through the world, pressing his skinny body against things he wanted to understand. I watched him press up against Arthur as we walked. Arthur moved aside the first couple of times, until he realized the touch was a gesture and not an accident. Then he went on as though Jo-Jo were not walking beside him, close as a shadow, as though Jo-Jo had not taken him by the hand as an apprehensive child his father's in a place of confusion.

We all bunched up at the gate and paid our money, and as we gathered on the other side, this lady snapped our photo. What a gaggle of misfits! Autumn chill hid some of our individuality under overcoats, but there was Alamo's inevitable dirt blue ski-cap (evident summer, winter, bed, shower—though he didn't shower that often); there were Carnage's ripped-to-shreds, true-to-his-name army surplus khakis hung with military memorabilia; there was Jo-Jo with one big flannel shirt flapping around his fencepost body, as though the bones and skin that made up most of him didn't feel the cold. And there were Arthur and me, looking pretty normal, I thought, though Arthur had worn a bright red shirt and I was so extraordinarily handsome that it did rather jar the eye.

I'd worried about who would dominate the crew (I meant to, if it came to that), but the surprise and wonder of the place were so great that we just naturally wandered around in a clump, babes-in-the-woods style, taking it all in together. It provided a form of protection, I guess, as well as a portable chorus for our observations. One theme pervaded. As Jo-Jo remarked, "They're all dressed like Mee-Maw's Mee-Maw." Most of the employees were, in fact, got up as old-time mountain people in bonnets and buckskins. There were coonskin caps and bolts of gingham and jugs with three *x*'s on them, which were meant to allude to moonshine. But it was Christmas, too, so there was an intermingling Victorian theme: top hats and big elaborate dresses, and one tall gent going around muttering, "Bah, humbug!"

Arthur said, "They're not missing a trick, are they?"

It was true that somebody had made sure that whatever memory you had of Christmas, whatever rumor came to you from the Christmases of your grandmothers back in the coves under the mountains, whatever echoes remained from a production of *The Christmas Carol* you played Bob Cratchit in during middle school, it was represented in the shops and walkways of Dollywood, hung with lights and ablaze with tinsel. Arthur in particular seemed awestruck. "There's no principle of selection," he said. "It's like . . . you know what it's like?"

"No," Carnage responded, really interested. "What's it like?"

"It's like if some big disaster came upon us, a release of toxic gas or all the volcanoes in the world exploding at once, and we were pretty much wiped out, every man, woman, and child on the earth gone, except it was Christmas, you know, Christmas Eve, and a few malls were left standing out in the boondocks, a few malls out in Nebraska or Arkansas or something, all decorated up for Christmas. Then ten years or so later aliens land—"

"Aliens?" Alamo chimed in. "Aliens from where?"

"From Uranus," Carnage responded, inevitably. We all laughed, and Arthur got on with his proposition.

"Suppose these aliens—from Uranus—landed, and all they could find was these malls full up with crap to buy and all decorated up for Christmas. Then one day they decided to build a museum dedicated to Earth Before the Great Disaster. This is what they would build. Having only the Christmas malls out in the boondocks to go on, Dollywood is what they would come up with."

I saw Jo-Jo peering around with his blue lips, and his red hands jammed into his pockets. He was considering Arthur's speech, nodding slowly, gravely, his mop of unruly hair cascading down his inclined forehead. He said, very slowly, very distinctly, "Mother fucker." It was a kind of "amen."

Dolly herself was singing "Go Tell It on the Mountain" from a loudspeaker hidden in the crotch of a tree. All the people who had been poor and ignorant and miserable in real life were here transformed into Christmas gnomes, jolly and fragrant, offering the myriad comforts, manning the near-infinity of cash registers. All you needed was a credit card, and everyone had that. Dolly was the one who had made it out. Dolly was the goddess who had passed through fire and death, through paparazzi and face lifts, through Nashville and Hollywood, then turned back with her arms full of bounty, blessing and forgiving, transfiguring the past so that everyone who had come out of those dead coal mines and exhausted farms could imagine that they had traveled the same road and arrived at the same place as she. She had given them salvation that did not change what they were, but implied that what they were was plenty good enough, could its credos be sung in harmony sweet enough, could Jesus be thanked and welcomed by them often enough, could it all be powdered with enough glitter. Dolly was a Moses who marched the masses out of Egypt and back to Egypt again in a tight little loop going nowhere, but changing Egypt in the meanwhile into a Canaan hung with colored lights and peopled by figures out of books, so that you could think you had the whole while been sojourning to the Promised Land.

Mee-Maw smashed the last hard autumn apples into mush to spread on your bread through the winter, but you could buy nine-dollar Tahitian Island preserves that were supposed to be just like home because there was a picture of a crone in a sunbonnet stirring jelly on a woodfire stove on the snow-white label. Mee-Maw saved her pennies for milk for the baby, but you could idle in mile-long lines and buy a new coat for three dollars less at the Eddie Bauer outlet store.

The theme park around us celebrated all that: thrift that was still thrift though it went forth in a jangle of unnecessary possessions, country values that were still country values even if you brought them out for Thanksgiving and Christmas only, piety that was still piety even though it was aimed at a sixteen-year-old Santa Christ leading the parade of toy soldiers into Toyland.

As if he had been listening to my thoughts, Jo-Jo muttered again, "Mother fucker," leaning against the tree Dolly was singing in, trying through his cold skin and raw bones to understand.

We were glad for the rides and coasters. They had themes, too—runaway coal cars and haunted mines—but you could ignore the themes and just ride. They were neutral, exciting, like the modern world, like my world. I thought about this. I wondered what if the aliens came and found only my dorm room left, and tried to construct a world out of that. Empty bottles would assume an inordinate centrality. If my hard drive survived, they might assume everybody was naked and looked like Pamela Anderson. I hoped we weren't in a wreck on 40 that night. I longed to get back to the room in time to change, or at least to enrich, the memory of our world before the volcanos cast finality over all.

Jo-Jo had no stomach for rides, and he stood with his hands jammed in his pockets and his neck lowered down into his shoulders, stamping around against the cold while we rode. I was glad for that, actually, glad to have something to look at—the way a dancer spots on a single place so she doesn't puke—as we spun and overturned. Jo-Jo as the center of my world was not what I'd anticipated, but there you are.

And I did vomit, copiously, carefully, under the pine trees that were probably planted there for that purpose, and the taste was taken away by the cotton candy that Jo-Jo had ready for me when we staggered off the big coasters. That was the confirmation I'd wanted, and it was comforting, despite everything. The trip was a success for me.

Alamo said I was the only one in the whole park throwing up. I didn't believe him, but even if it were true, it made me special in some way I would be able to figure out before I rode my next ride.

Night is beautiful in Dollywood: all the trees become Christmas trees, all the buildings lined with blue and red fire, a parade made of long-eared elves and giant mice driving crazy cars winding through at the appointed hour. The evening hours of our visit found us dazed and exhausted, but we held on, wanting to drink that cup to the very dregs. We had long since stopped talking with our first excited energy, too, except for Alamo, who was ride-mad and kept extolling the virtues of this or that brand of centrifugal peril. At the end we all stood with Jo-Jo on the pavement while Alamo got in one last turn on the coaster. I admired him. He was happy. He jogged in circles around us like a puppy, and though the park was closing, he kept gazing back wistfully at the wheels and parabolas glittering in the purple air. I think he had missed the philosophical discussion that so colored our perception of Dollywood. I think he was waiting in line for the Mystery Mine the second or third time. Power to him.

Slight rearrangement was necessary on the way home. I retained shotgun because of my knee, but Alamo was moved from the middle of the backseat to one of the windows. Alamo did not customarily use toiletries, and after a day like we'd had, it began to show, and it was important to have him to one side so the smell was as little pervasive as it could be. Alamo knew he smelled and initiated the change himself, so there were no hard feelings. He kept his window cracked the whole way, which was okay because we preferred the draft to Alamo's worn-a-little-too-long T-shirt. He was revved up about the rides, so he chattered on a little after we hit the road, admiring me because I rode and puked and yet rode again, but before the lights of Pigeon Forge faded, we had all subsided into a going-home-after-a-long-day stupor. Carnage, who had violent clothing but a clear conscience, was asleep almost immediately, scrunched up against Jo-Jo in a way that, for Jo-Jo, was a form of conversation.

Jo-Jo said, "When my dad was driving cross country he never stopped. We had to hold our pee and all that because he never stopped."

"Why?"

"Dad said there were monsters. Out in the darkness there were monsters and if you were alone on a long road, they lost their fear and came at you."

"He just didn't want to stop."

Jo-Jo shrugged. He said, "There are more things in heaven and on earth, Horatio." We were all glad we went to college.

The homeward road lay dark and bare, the world become rolling black hills against an almost black sky, stabbed here and there by the lights of houses or isolated strip malls. Deer stood on the roadside, wise deer who waited for us to pass before they darted out on their swift nocturnal ways. Way out at the end of driveways, barn doors were lit up by greenish nightlights. Dogs barked. If anyone had ever been alone on an isolated road, it was us on this one. From the sounds of breathing I guessed everyone in back was asleep. Arthur slipped a disk in, and at first my innards tightened with disappointment. It was classical. He was driving, though, and it was his right to pick the music, and he had, after all, waited 'til everyone was asleep to indulge himself in this secret preference. He set the music low, and it amazed me to find myself poking the volume button a few times to hear it better.

"Bach," Arthur said. "Bach was a—"

"I know who Bach was. Why the hell did you pick—"

"Everybody's asleep. It's soothing."

Ba da da da da Ba da da da da—

It wasn't soothing me. I know I sounded gruff, but it was a long day, and the throw-up had burned my throat a little. But I listened. The song was long—ten, twenty times longer than a song on my iPod—but it was still one piece, an entity, rolling out, unfolding in the comfortably smelly dimness of the car. It was a song nobody was singing, of course, violins and . . . and lots of other stuff. God, I was ignorant. I didn't know what I was hearing. What the principle of it was. I could have asked Arthur, but the tone was set already, the tone of sleep and secret thoughts, and I was not going to break it for that. Arthur's hand reached for the eject button, and his voice said, "Do you want me to—" But I said, "No. Leave it." I wanted it to sound like a concession, but it was really a request. I wanted to hear. I didn't understand what I was hearing, or why it affected me as it did. It was the opposite of Dollywood. I knew that, but if Dr. Einstadt from philosophy were in the car demanding that I be able to explain, I would have flunked in an instant.

"Does anybody ever sing?"

"Oh yes, of course, there are cantatas for every—"

I waved my hand to make him stop. It was meant as a criticism rather than an inquiry. Arthur could be very exhausting. He didn't pick up the cues.

The unaccustomed music moved me, and I didn't know why. Even minus words it was *about* something in a way most of my tunes were not. It was a lecture, only the lecturer didn't care if you were listening, and nobody took attendance. It was information. It was one side of a conversation, waiting for me to respond, which I would have had I known how. The strings said, *Riley . . . Riley. . .* calling my name with that little upward lilt they had. I could hear them, but I didn't know how to answer. I wished there were a book somewhere where all this was written out. Maybe there was. I couldn't believe my own ignorance. I'd ask Arthur when the spell was off.

"Riley?"

Arthur's voice sounded resonant and portentous in the dark.

"Yeah?"

"I thought it was awful. Horrendous. Terrifying."

"What was? *Dollywood?*"

"Yeah. I'm sorry. I just don't get it."

"You don't get it?"

"You could help me."

A succession of white slashes passed under the car, lit by the lonely blaze of headlights. I didn't know what to say

"I figured you could take the news. The others . . . It would be like telling them there is no Santa Claus. Though, in fact, I've never been convinced about that one. You know my dad still sneaks into the living room Christmas Eve after I've gone to bed and hangs up a stocking on the same old nail?"

"No, I didn't know that, Arthur."

"You pissed at me?"

"I've always admitted that you're way smarter than me. This is the first time you've used that intelligence to mock something I hold sacred."

I could feel Arthur deflating from across the seat.

"Oh, Christ, I didn't mean that at all—"

"I know. Just let me sit here and think for a moment."

Arthur released a long sigh and glued his face back onto the winding Tennessee road before us.

I'd impressed myself with my passionate—if a little disingenuous—defense of Dollywood. I didn't want to say anything else. Truth was, I found it disappointing, too, but that attitude was a kind of betrayal, a kind of uppityness I didn't like finding in myself. Dolly held her arms out to you, palms up, glittering with treats and souvenirs. If you hungered for something to eat, she would rustle it up. Dolly told you that the way you always were was good enough. She said, "Come on over, darlin'. I know what you wanted, and I suppose that's what you'll always want, and I got plenty of it."

Arthur's CD made no reference to anything like that. Johann Sebastian said, "I'm as unlike Dollywood as anything you can imagine." He wanted me to make a choice, him or it, but I wasn't prepared. Not that night in that car, with Jo-Jo's monsters racing alongside us waiting for their chance. I was thinking so hard I didn't notice when my belly began to ache. Arthur heard me rustling in my seat.

"Your stomach still upset from the rides?"

He wanted to know if he had to pull over. I said, "A little. But I'm all right."

Five seconds later I said, as firmly as I could. "Pull over. Now."

I don't know what it was I was still throwing up. Everything that went down had come up already, so I thought. But my body was finding ammunition somewhere, and when that ran out, there I was bent over at midnight in the wilderness, dry heaving with a sound that, itself, made one sick. Ribbons of junk were hanging out of my mouth, the way it does, and Arthur was handing me tissues to take care of it. The headlights beamed into the distance, across a field of some low silage crop glittering with frost. The lights went a really long way and hit, so I thought, the pitched roof of a shed at the far end of the field.

When I reached back to take another tissue, I heard something that was not the sound of my own retching. In the dark close by, out of the range of the headlights and far enough away not to be lit by the open car door, something was moving. Had to be a cow or an old farm dog or something, but the sound was wrong. Whatever body had made it was not . . . was not familiar to me. My stomach wanted another go, but I held it off long enough to peer into the darkness. Perhaps something had been attracted to the sound of my sickness, the way predators are drawn to the sick and the weak. I held my breath. I could feel the acid run upwards on the inside of my throat, but if I were vomiting fire, I would have held it off to get a clear view of what moved toward me in the darkness. Bach was still playing inside. It was sinister now, metallic and precise, like the flight of an arrow. It didn't care about me. As I bent over to have another go, I saw eyes appear at the edge between dark and light, eyes kindled by the headlights, four, six, high off the ground, higher than a deer, higher than a man. Behind them were dark masses, big bodies, massive and built wrong for the normal things I knew, hesitating that final moment, deciding just then whether to lurk or to dash suddenly into the light.

"*Go! Go! Go!*" I was screaming, slamming the door behind me. I'd frightened Arthur so bad it took him a second to remember how to drive, and in that second something came out of the field that had been given back to the dark by the shutting of the car door. I felt something touch the handle. I was screaming and pushing against Arthur to get as far from the door as I could. The guys in back were wide awake now, looking around for the wreck we must have been in to cause all that furor.

"*Go! Go! Go!*"

Arthur spun the tires on the wet grass and finally made it to the road. He eased off a little until I screamed *Go!* I looked back through the open window. Alamo peered back through his window, too, looking up alternately at me for some clue as to what the fuck the matter was.

"What the—"

"There was something out there."

Someone in the backseat began to snicker. They were taking it as a joke. They thought I had started screaming the way you do in the dark just to scare the piss out of your buddies.

Carnage said, "That was a good one."

Arthur had made a couple of sharp turns on the winding road. He said, "It's the goddamn CD. That's the problem now. The goddamn Bach." He hit the eject button. There was midnight quiet, filled only by the sounds of innocent sleepers in the dark behind.

Carnage lived off campus and was the first to be let off. Jo-Jo elbowed him a couple of times, until he gathered his tattered khakis around him and rolled out of the backseat. He stood for a moment, rubbing his eyes like a sleepy child. Someone in the house had kept the light on for him. We backtracked a little toward campus. Arthur found a parking spot near the dorms, and we piled out. Arthur stood with the back door open to air it out a little after Alamo disappeared into the night. He reached into his pocket and pulled out a roll of mints. I took a couple. My breath must have been awful.

"We didn't make bad time."

"No."

"What time is it, anyway?"

"Fuck the time. What was all that back there?"

"Art, I saw something. Out in the field when I was—I saw something."

Arthur was quiet for a while, and then he said, "You know, Dollywood wasn't a complete bust. There were things I liked."

"Yeah, what?"

Very slowly, as though it were a poem and he was explicating it for class, he said, "That blue tree. The sycamore hung with lights, so at sunset, before it was really dark and you could tell they were lights, you thought it was really a blue tree. That had me. I was standing far away at first trying to figure out what kind it was. Trying to remember what country had trees like that, and what would a forest look like, and how could I get there. Blue. Weird winter blue. I liked that."

"Arthur, you are a piece of work."

"So you say. You feeling better?"

"Yeah."

I gathered my things up. Arthur helped me. I guess I was still a little sick. We were in separate dorms. I regretted this, because I didn't want to be alone in the dark the length of time it took me to get to mine.

"You want me to walk you home?"

"Yeah."

I was relieved to have Arthur beside me. The night was sweet and, for a college campus, quiet. When we were almost at my door Arthur said, "I saw them, too."

"The monsters? Out in the field?"

The look on his face was strange. He shrugged and said, "Monsters? That's not what I saw. I watched them in the starlight crossing the field, the whole time you were sick. The great, strange bodies. I thought maybe they heard the Bach . . . maybe they were coming . . . so I could see them, just this once. Their kind."

His voice turned down at the end with such theatrical sadness I looked at him to see if he was joking. He wasn't. Arthur play-punched me in the jaw and then turned his back, heading toward his sleep with that little behind-the-back wave he had, which was sadder and more ambiguous at midnight than he probably understood. I wanted to call after him. I wanted to settle the matter of the creatures in the field. But I was afraid, standing there by myself, afraid even to call out lest the wrong thing hear. I punched in my code and opened the door.

How to Play Your Hand in Little Tokyo

Evan Hundhausen

"LET ME IN AND THE GAME WILL BEGIN," I SAY INTO THE INTERCOM WHEN I arrive at a five-story building sitting directly across from Japanese Village Plaza in Little Tokyo off East 2nd Street in Los Angeles to attend an illegal poker room at six in the morning.

The lobby has no doorman. Just white walls with typical apartment slot-style mailboxes lining one side. I'm buzzed in, see the elevator, step inside of it, and take it to the third floor. I exit the flying metal box finally and pass by a nice table piece in the hall, just sitting there, having no purpose but to look elegant and antique-like in this hallway. Above the table, hanging on the wall, is an art piece done by the late Andy Warhol. I don't know which work of art this one is called per se, and in the end it is just a poster and not the real thing of course, not *real* art, but it's a *real* colorful piece. If you saw it, you'd know which one I was talking about, but in the end I don't even stop to admire it and keep walking down the hallway until I arrive at apartment 300B.

I knock on the door with my knuckles, and a large Asian man opens it, standing there, filling up the whole doorway with his large sumo-like body. In fact, it's easy to imagine him wearing a thong, squatting in some dirt sumo arena somewhere, all ready to go belly-to-belly with somebody who's just as big as him, but this is not a pretty picture, so I try to think of something else fast, like this game I'm about to play: Texas Hold'em Poker.

"Hi," I say to the giant standing before me. The sumo guy has a buzz haircut, wears a black suit, and has shiny black shoes to match. "Where do you shop, man? Your feet are so goddamned big!"

I expect him to grunt like those sumo-sized Asians always do in TV shows and old James Bond movies, but instead he takes a few steps back to let me inside the room. Maybe he doesn't know English. I admire his shirt next, the one he's wearing under his black suit, a red-collared button-up with one of those western cowboy, slipknot, tie-knot, string-tie-things. Now I'm thinking this man must have some Native American blood in him if he's sporting all this, so I ask him, "Are you part Native American, dude?"

His eyes narrow and he looks at me like he doesn't know what I'm talking about, bent brow and all, shaking his head *no* in the negative and making a grunt (*Finally!*). Bodyguards are funny in that way. They never smile, and I'm sure it's in their job description not to.

He motions for me to step inside the apartment and then frisks me down with his thick, square-shaped-fingered hands that look like that character from the *Fantastic Four*. I just can't think of that *thing's* name . . .

"Good evening, Mr. Benjamins!" says a voice with an accent, coming from inside the room. It's another Japanese man walking toward me in a swift, brisk manner. He can't be more than five feet tall, and he's wearing another black suit. We're all wearing black suits, actually. Even me. This large sumo bodyguard standing next to this shorter man is a sight to see if you can imagine.

I realize the short Japanese man has said my name in the plural, so I say to him, "You can call me Ben." Then I say, "Your suit looks like mine, *Flash!* Giorgio Armani?"

He nods in agreement, but I don't know if he's agreeing with me or if he doesn't understand me. The hand he shakes mine with has more than one gold ring on his fingers.

"Look at those rings!" I continue talking because I had a triple shot latte this morning and I'm out of control. "I never wear rings because I always feel it gets in the way when I'm using my hands, and in this game I use my hands a lot, know what I mean, Flash?"

The short man ignores me again, smiling. He holds out his other arm pointing in the direction of the poker table in this large apartment I'm in. The ceiling must go twenty feet up and the room is dark, only lit by the morning light coming from several large windows with heavy red curtains covering them. I can see dust particles in the air where the early morning sun strikes through the slits of the curtains casting light onto the wooden floor that creaks when I follow this short man to the table.

I remember talking to Flash over the phone. I remember his accent. He kept telling me how excited everyone was about me coming. It's always nice to be wanted even if it's just another freaking poker game in the end. Walking ahead of me the bottoms of his black pant legs make a swishing sound as he heads toward the poker table already filled with the other players.

"Am I late?" I ask.

"You are on time, Mr. Benjamins," he says.

"Please, call me Ben," I state again, unable to help pointing this out one more time. "Although *Benjamins* isn't that bad of a name. Reminds me of one-hundred-dollar bills, and that's a good thing, so maybe you're my lucky charm calling me that, Flash."

The man takes a moment to look at me quizzically but smiles again. I wonder if he understands my joking around and about me giving him the nickname *Flash* and all. Maybe he doesn't and I should just stop it and ask him his real name instead.

The first person I notice at the table is a man holding a newspaper up, covering his whole face while he reads it. On the front page the headline for today, Tuesday, October 28, 1997, is *Wall Street Washed Out! Dow Dives 554 Led by Asian Markets!*

My brother and I were just talking about the stock market last week and he said to me, "You need savings, man. You need a retirement plan."

He's a fiduciary and likes these crazy things called annuities where you make like 7 percent or more off your money every year. The thing about it is, if the stock market goes down, like it did today, you don't lose your shirt, and when it goes up you make even more per year in return. They sound all right, really, if you're retired and all.

"You're going to have to start saving all that money you're making at those poker rooms," he said to me as if it's any of his business. I told him I didn't know how to do that, and he said to just ask a mobster the next time I'm sitting next to one during a poker hand.

Funny, my brother is, and I remember telling him, "Why would I ask a thug how to save money, or for any advice at all for that matter? Brother, what you don't realize is I don't make friends with any of the people I play games with. Casual conversation is made, but if I started asking criminals how they do business, then all of a sudden I'd be in their business, too, and the mob's not a business I desire to be in, capiche?" But in the end I told my brother, "Don't worry about me. My savings is under my mattress, so as long as nobody knows where I live, I'm in business."

My apartment is in my girlfriend's mother's name. I rent two neighboring apartments in Metuchen, New Jersey—one for me and my girl and one for her mom. We live a couple blocks away from the Amtrak station. Lots of times you can find me with a coffee and newspaper in hand, coming home after playing a game all night and it'll be seven or eight o'clock in the morning and I'm arriving at the Metuchen stop. It's like I'm coming home from work while everyone else on the train is going. I play poker like someone would work overtime at their 9 to 5 job. I've done sixty to one hundred hours a week before, all hours of the day and night. Mostly night, but you know how it is. The house always wins, but sometimes I do because I know how to make the averages work out in my favor.

Really, I'm not kidding.

It's not rocket science to find an illegal poker room, either. If you hang out in Atlantic City a lot or go to a local off-track betting place, you can meet people with big mouths, talking about these places because people talk, but otherwise you can ask any taxi driver because once they get done telling you about prostitutes they'll tell you about a gambling house or two and what street it's on and of course they'll even drive you up there and drop you off.

Normally I'll arrive in Penn Station and catch the C train riding it up past 125th going into neighborhoods like Harlem or even the Bronx. I've found myself in not so nice places, but then I've also found myself in unimaginably elegant, high-end places, all over, uptown, midtown, Chinatown, and even in Brooklyn.

When I frequent illegal rooms, sometimes, I'll even see celebrities from the TV and they'll have wads of cash they want to lose. Several weeks ago I recognized a guy at a secret club in Uptown Manhattan. I'd seen him on the cast of *Saturday Night Live* the night before. The skit he was in made me laugh a lot.

I can see the man sitting at the table with the newspaper covering his face is missing his pointer finger on his left hand. He's someone I know and is a friend of mine.

"Joey Nine Fingers!" I say, and he looks over the newspaper at me through his oversized tortoiseshell glasses and smiles.

I've never been in a raid and that's because I can get the skinny if a place is going to get shut down in advance from Joey Nine Fingers, who knows a crapload about which spots are on the cops' radar and which ones are not. He's one of the few people I know in the scene that has my personal phone number, and he'll leave me a message or page me. I'll go down to a payphone because I'm kind of paranoid in that way, just am, and he'll tell me not to go to a certain place because it's going to get raided. How he knows this, *who knows?* but I'm lucky he fills me in, so I can stay in business for myself.

"Yeah, don't go to Manny's no more. He's shut down! He must have done something to piss somebody off. Too bad. I liked that hostess that worked there. Mindy? *Gawd.* She's hot," and after conversations like these I'll say, "Thanks for the tip, Joey-Niner," and go on with my crazy life.

Joey looks over the top of the newspaper and he's smiling mischievously. He folds it up and places it neatly on the table. He's happy to see me and I am, too. He points at me with his left hand that's missing his pointer finger, if you can imagine that. He's a joker. Joey-Nine lost his finger from a table saw, cutting a piece of plywood. He hasn't really told me the full story of his finger getting cut off, it must've sucked, but once he said something like it was a *relief* and honestly, I don't really know what he meant by that, but I'm sure it had to do with some Buddhist philosophy about *loss*, like how can you be a poker player if you can't get used to *loss*?

It's impossible, I tell ya.

I sit down at the table and greet the person sitting next to me. He's the man who invited me here in the first place, Jen Zen Iotonka, a man who owns multiple island resorts around the world, but his most famous one is out in the Fiji Islands. Maybe you saw the writeup in *Condé Nast* last month? I did because my girlfriend bought a copy and left the magazine lying out on the coffee table at home.

The Fiji Islands look like a great place to go spend quality time when you see all the pictures in the magazine. In these bungalows there are no walls and there's a view of the water from the straw-roofed villas you stay in. Celebrities like Robert DeNiro, Liz Taylor, and others go to places like this, and the price per night is astronomical.

Jen Zen says hello to me, even stands up and bows, so I feel obligated to bow back.

"He's been doing that to everybody," says one of the players at the table. I look over at who's said this.

"It's the famous Eddie Pool!" I say, greeting him.

"You meant to say infamous." He frowns.

"I read that book you wrote cover to cover," I tell him.

"Well, I'm scared now. You know all my tricks."

People laugh at his comment, and I look around the table at the other players here for the game. There's six all together including myself. One of them is Lonnie Dolls, who I've played with once before, and she likes to wear sunglasses, a baseball cap, and a spandex outfit that shows off her body. She's quite a distraction if you know what I mean. The other person there is someone I've never met before and I say hi to him and introduce myself.

The short Japanese man, Flash, asks me if I would like coffee. Then a man dressed in all white like he's a chef walks out of the back kitchen area, through a swinging door, carrying coffee, cream, and sugar on a tray. I say yes to the coffee and it is poured in front of me from a silver pitcher. It's all very foo-foo what's happening and better than being in some dump back in New York. I've found myself spending hours playing poker games in places where you'll see a cockroach crawling up a wall or a rat sitting in a dark corner for no good reason. Not cool being in those places, especially when you're trying to concentrate on your hand.

Today I'm in for the long haul. We're starting at 6:15 a.m. on the dot, and it's a strange time to start playing poker, but no matter, all of us here could literally go all day playing if we're not careful and then all freaking night if we wanted to. Playing for twenty-four hours straight has happened to me once or twice. Usually you take a break, but sometimes not. Sometimes you don't know if the sun is up or down depending what kind of room you're in. It's full-on-no-joke-poker and everyone here, no doubt, is out for blood like I am. The winner will walk out with almost $100,000 today.

I had to buy in with $16,500 last week. Five hundred goes to the house or Jen Zen's pocket. I had to meet a man in Manhattan to give him the buy-in money. It was sketch, but that's the way it goes. It's not like I wanted him to come to my house to pick it up. It'd be easier to overnight it or bank wire, but whatever, I have to do what I gotta do. The parking lot was in some abandoned lot that used to be a factory or something. I had to turn my headlights on and off to signal to the other car, the only one there when I drove up. It was like a drug deal or something, and he turned his headlights on and off in his black Cherokee with tinted windows. There were two guys in that car, not anyone here, but more big, sumo-looking Asian dudes. I gave them a bag with my money in it and they drove off and that's how I bought into the game.

There's a dealer standing in front of us at this green poker table we're all sitting at. He's an official Texas Hold'em dealer from Las Vegas. Several of the players obviously know him from the way they're talking to him all chummy. He stands there playing with the cards like he's going to perform some magic card tricks at any moment dressed in that typical casino uniform.

WE STARTED OUR FIRST game and the short man who called me Benjamins informed us how the air conditioning isn't working. "We're going to try to remedy this situation as fast as possible," he said and then explained how they're going to buy some fans from a store to bring back up here. The sumo wrestler bouncer was given instructions and exited the apartment to go buy those fans.

"I guess we can't cancel the game since you flew in from Japan and all," said Joey Nine Fingers to Jen Zen our host.

"I'm so sorry," Jen Zen said looking at Joey and then at all of us. "Please forgive me for this unfortunate circumstance."

Lonnie Dolls stated the obvious. "It's not a problem because I came to play."

"What an advantage you have," Eddie Pool told her. "It seems like you're the only one dressed for the occasion," meaning her spandex and the air conditioning being out, and everyone laughed at Eddie's remark.

Now we're playing our umpteenth hand in this hot room and Eddie starts talking about something interesting. Something I've never heard before. He mentions the name of some Jewish man. Everyone around the table seems to know who Eddie is talking about but me.

"He made the jingle for the Transformers toys, didn't he?" says Joey.

"I don't know about that," Eddie says, "but I was talking to him the other day at a tournament and he told me he just invented something ingenious. It's a camera that can see hole cards under the table. The poker table will have glass, so the camera under it can show TV viewers the hole cards all the players at the table have. Apparently there's going to be a poker TV show coming out in Europe somewhere airing it for the first time. Soon, it'll be everywhere and it'll be huge. There'll be more poker fans than ever. The tournaments in Vegas will get bigger and the pots will get larger, too!"

"No one wants to watch poker on TV," Lonnie comments, faking a yawn. "Boring."

"Yeah, they'd rather watch baseball or something," Joey-Nine says.

I start realizing I've never played in a tournament in Vegas, but it sounds like I should think about it from what Eddie Pool's saying.

"Your name is more suitable for a pool shark, don't you think, Eddie?" I say, changing the subject like the professional that I am. You gotta work every psychological angle on these guys. "A last name like yours? You should be hustling pool like Paul Newman in that movie."

"Ha," he says. "Never heard that one before."

Then Eddie starts talking about his family tree and how an ancestor of his was a pool shark, but I'm still trying to imagine these hole card cameras he was just talking about and I'm looking down at the green poker table visualizing a video camera pointing up at my cards that are facedown, recording it all from underneath the table and through the glass, so people on TV can follow the action. It's something trying to imagine all that.

Me on TV? Yeah. Right.

THE HOURS PASS. HANDS are dealt and hands are folded.

I've basically been playing poker for five hours now. We took a break at 11 a.m., and a huge spread of different dishes supplied from a local Japanese restaurant was delivered up for us to eat. I could've taken a nap after that, but no sleep for me, I still have money to win off these bums.

Jen Zen has shown how great he is at losing. I've been watching him grimace every time he loses a hand. I played the obvious psychological advantage early on. The air conditioner was out for a long time and since arriving in LA it's been 90 or 100 degrees this week, unseasonably hot. Eddie Pool pulled out his handkerchief early on and he's been wiping his brow ferociously the whole time.

"When are they coming back with those fans?" he's been complaining miserably.

Joey Nine Fingers has been using his missing finger to his advantage, pointing at people with his nub when he makes small talk. Then he'll put it to his nose like he's really digging for gold, but there's no finger there, so he's not really picking it.

I know personally, when I look at his missing finger, sometimes I can feel a pang of shock run through my body, but I know him so well it doesn't bother me anymore, but for people who don't know him, it may distract them just enough, and Joey ain't no fool playing this up to his advantage. He even makes sure he's holding the cards or betting with his chips with the hand with the missing pointer finger, so everyone can get a glimpse at it.

One time he told me, "I sometimes get an itch and it's in the spot where my finger's missing." I couldn't imagine experiencing a phantom limb, but that's Joey's life.

He's my only friend in this poker world I play in, the only buddy I have here, but let's get back to *my* advantage. I'm winning huge today from the fact that there's no air conditioning.

I'll tell ya a story, now. You see, this one time I went on a fishing ship with my friend from high school. We'd gone down to the Jersey shore, paid a fee, and got on a commercial boat. These fishing boats are cool because they do everything for you from supplying the poles, baiting it for you, and then cleaning and dressing the fish you catch, so all you have to do is take it home to eat. The only problem was my friend and I weren't used to being on boats this size, smaller, not like no cruise ship, and we both got seasick. I can still see him groaning and lying on the wooden bench inside the ship cabin. I was feeling ill too because of the unending up and down motion of the fishing boat, but suddenly I realized I've paid for this experience, so I might as well get back to the fishing. I got up from the bench and started to have a really good time then.

Sometimes the lines would get caught in someone else's, like from the guy standing next to ya, so I would let my line slack and let it go out farther than everyone else's, gauging how far my line should go by seeing all the others zip around the surface of the ocean, all baited by the assistants on board to catch those fish. I figured if my line went out farther than the rest of everybody else it would be less obvious for the fish to realize they're gonna get hooked. I caught a couple that way and brought them back home after to eat, real proud of myself.

"Enjoy eating all the mercury," my friend said, smoking a cigarette. He'd spent the whole time in the cabin being seasick and not fishing at all.

So, basically, no air conditioning is totally to my advantage today. While everyone took their suit coats off, unbuttoning their collars and sweating at their armpits, I raked in the money by getting in the *zone* and not thinking about how uncomfortable it all was. You can't beat days like this, and you have to take advantage of every angle in this crazy game to win.

THE FANS WERE BROUGHT in and turned on late in the day. Apparently the sumo bouncer got lost in traffic. Now, it's 3 p.m. and the last hand. There are just three of us left at the table, still playing, while everyone else, who's lost, smokes cigarettes and watches.

I go all in because I figure both Lonnie Dolls and Eddie Pool are bluffing. When you play poker and want to be successful at it there are times when you have to risk going all in. There are two kings sitting on the table face up, the community cards, and I have the other two kings in my hand. Four of a kind is a great hand and I have to go all in. The only thing that'll beat it is a straight flush: five cards in consecutive order and all in the same suit. Now, there's an ace community card sitting there on the table, too, and maybe someone holds two aces, but one of them, Lonnie or Eddie, is bluffing for sure.

I know they both don't mind bluffing after seeing them do it a couple times from playing with them all day long like I have. Lonnie even showed everyone a crappy hand she had after she won from bluffing just for spite. I filed that away in the back of my mind. Then there is the book Eddie Pool wrote with the chapter devoted to nothing but bluffing, which I've read and re-read several times, so logic says I need to take this chance and go balls to the wall and all in.

In the end Eddie has aces, three of a kind, and Lonnie has nothing, and I don't know why she went all in like that. She could've folded. Maybe the heat got to her? Don't really know, but I've won! $16,000 times six is . . . I don't know, but Jen Zen bows to me and leaves the room in a hurry. Maybe it's back to Japan for him. Then Flash shakes my hand. "Congratulations, Mr. Benjamins."

"Call me Ben," I tell him again.

Joey Nine Fingers walks up to me and puts his good hand out to shake mine.

"Good game, you lucky bastard!"

"Yeah, yeah," I say. "Next time it'll be you that wins."

"You're right. I will!" He laughs a hearty laugh and slaps me on the back. "You lucky bastard," he says again. "Good to see you. I'm taking the next flight out. This place is too hot. I hate LA."

"You're supposed to *love* LA," I say, referring to that song with the same title, and Joey-Nine walks off smiling.

BACK AT THE HOTEL I meet my girlfriend and she asks me if I need a change of clothes or even a nap. I have a large backpack with my winnings in it strapped to my shoulders and I'm sure I look like a high school student with it on.

"Aren't you going to leave your bag in the room?"

"Heck no, it stays with me," I tell my girlfriend, Amika, who's overly concerned about nothing, but that's why I like her.

It's like sometimes you realize no one cares about you at all. You're going through life alone and then you meet someone who actually *does* care and you have no choice but to make her your girlfriend because you know what it's like without all that, at least that's how I see it.

We walk across the street from the hotel and hit the Japanese Village in Little Tokyo because Amika wants to shop and that's no problem since I got a bag of money around my shoulders. One store we enter has nothing but lady products and she buys some crazy shit, lots of mud masks and cosmetic things all made in Japan. Then she picks up some weird pads you put on your feet at night to take out the toxins while you sleep.

"If you wear that you're going to look and smell like Frankenstein, you know it? And I have to sleep with you to boot."

"Whatever, you snore," she states with a frown on her face for emphasis, "and I have to put up with that. Plus, no one's stopping you from sleeping on the couch, are they?"

"You're cold as ice," I say. "Speaking of ice, let's go get some ice cream or a frosty or something."

I grab her love handle and squeeze it hard, making her jerk away and laugh. We walk up to the cash register and I pull out a $100 bill from the roll I placed in my pocket earlier from my winnings.

"Why didn't you leave that bag at the hotel?" she asks again for some reason.

"Someone could steal it," I say.

"It's a five-star hotel. No one's going to steal it. The hotel even has a safe for customers."

"No thanks. I want to know where it is at all times," I tell her.

We're renting a car to drive home. All the way across the country. It's not like you can necessarily hide the money in a suitcase to take on a plane. Maybe you could, but a car ride home makes more sense for this adventure even though it takes longer. I usually don't bring my girlfriend along to poker games, but she's been begging for me to take her somewhere lately.

We exit the shop and walk along the sidewalk with all the other tourists that are outside today. I notice a black Jeep Cherokee with tinted windows pulling up along the curb. The yellow lights blink to double park there. I hear the electric, tinted window go down and I see it's the short man from back at the poker game. Flash, smiling at me like a criminal. What the fuck does he want?

"Mr. Benjamin," he begins talking to me out his window and he's said my name right this time. "An urgent matter has come to our attention and we'd like five minutes of your time."

"We?" Situations like this are inevitably sketch.

I look over at my girlfriend and behind her I see the sun beginning to set and there's pink in the sky. My girlfriend is decked out in the black outfit she bought yesterday in Beverly Hills. We visited some store owned by a clothing designer she read about in *Vogue* or *Cosmopolitan*, I've no idea, but she did and going to this boutique made her happy and seeing her happy makes me happy, but right now, she ain't happy. I can see it in her face.

"My girl and I are going to dinner, Flash," I say. "It's kind of inconvenient, right now."

"I understand, Mr. Benjamin. I assure you we will only inconvenience you for five minutes. We will drive around the block and drop you off exactly here, where we are picking you up. Your attendance to this matter is of the utmost importance and that is why I stress it to you in such an urgent manner. I hope you can forgive myself and Mr. Jen Zen for this inconvenience. You will be rewarded adequately for this delay to your dinner plans."

I see the guy do something suspect next. He's patting his suitcoat pocket very nonchalantly, like he's batting away a fly, but he's leaning forward out the window, so I will notice this gesture.

Now, this isn't the first time someone who's a sore loser has hunted me down after a game. There's been other times where the losing party was less cordial than this short Japanese man.

There's been other times where I've found a gun put to my head, like this one time down in Atlantic City. Security doesn't escort you to your car out there when you win big, like I hear they do in Las Vegas, and these two criminals followed me onto the Parkway and then when I pulled over to get some gas they pushed the barrel of a gun into my gut and made me get in their car. I'm just glad they didn't follow me all the way home where my girlfriend, her kid, and her mother would be.

Having a gun held to your head by the guy sitting behind you while you sit in the front passenger seat like you're in some movie, you get used to it only a little bit, if it's happened to you more than once maybe, but these sore losers ended up driving me out to Perth Amboy, to some deserted dock in a shipyard to scare me. They took the money I'd won and left me there without shoes, just my socks, and they took my pair of Air Jordans, like typical ghetto fucks, and it's a good thing I never saw them again because if I had . . . but they left me there and I didn't even have thirty-five cents to use a payphone, so I called Joey Nine Fingers collect. He wasn't home, so I begged for thirty-five cents off someone I happened to see when I started walking around Perth Amboy in my socks. It was easy to get the change because I looked pitiful.

"You should call the police, man!" the guy who gave me the change told me, but I said I wasn't going to do all that and I was okay and thanks for the thirty-five cents. I dialed Joey-Nine's pager and he called me back at the payphone I was standing at. Then he drove out to Perth Amboy and picked me up in his brown Studebaker. He took me to a seafood restaurant after, but first we stopped by a shoe store. *Strawberries* I think it was called.

Joey and I had some good laughs that day. You see, I can't really tell my girlfriend about stuff that happens to me out in this weird, wild world. She'd worry too much, so instead I got good ole' Joe to laugh about my troubles with.

"If I was there I would've taken care of both those punks." I remember Joey holding his hand out like he's making a gun with his pointer finger, but the joke is he's missing that finger and it's funny to watch him make fun of himself like that. Then there's the joke he played with our waitress. "Pull my finger," he told her, and she went wide-eyed seeing his missing finger like that and he laughed out loud putting her at ease.

Joey put the little fork with a bite of buttered lobster on it into his mouth. He'd been dipping the lobster in the butter ferociously and holding it up toward his lips like he was about to down the butter tub as if it was a shot of liquor. I remember little specks of butter splattered across his glasses even.

"It's better to give those jerks the money," I'd said. "They obviously need it more than I do. Plus, if I died who would take care of Amika and her kid?"

"I guess I would," Joey said sucking a lobster bone dry. "Those punk ass fucks will be dead within the week anyway. You can't act like that and expect to get away with it. It's a small town."

I thought of how Joey's wrong.

"It's not a small town," I'd said. "It's the Big Apple, the Empire State, and it's even New Jersey. It's called the metropolitan area and it's huge!"

"They'll end up in prison," he added, and I remember him spilling the butter on his shirt.

"Fuck!" he screamed unhappily. "This shirt is brand new!"

"It's just a shirt, Joe." I'd said. "You're making a commotion, Joey. Sit down! It's just a freaking shirt!"

I look at the short Japanese man's face sitting in the Jeep Cherokee there. I'm pissed that he's motioning to the gun in his blazer pocket. He's doing it all nonchalant like he's brushing lint off his suit, but I know what he's up to and he shouldn't be threatening me in front my girl.

I tell Amika that I will be right back and she pouts at me, but understands. I give her a kiss on the lips and walk toward the Jeep

Cherokee. The same sumo looking guy from the illegal game is the driver and he's gotten out of the car to open the door for me to get in. I'd like to tell both these jerks to take a hike, I really would, but it's all business and I have to go along or risk something worse happening, whatever that could be. It's not like I sit around thinking about what these goons do for a living when I'm not around.

I sit down next to Flash in the Jeep and think of what it would be like to take my two middle fingers and stick them both into his eyeballs, straight into them, full length, like they're screw drivers, so that my fingertips touch his brain and then I'd pull both fingers out of the cavities, so his messed-up eyeballs are stuck to them like kabobs. Then I'd start feeding them to him through his open mouth as he yells in agony in pain. He'd be blind and he could go back to Japan and be a dojo master like that blind monk in that old TV show *Kung Fu*, sitting in a hut dojo telling some David Carradine jerk that once he takes the pebble from his hand then it is time to graduate and leave the dojo, but when you really think about it, there really is no show at all until David Carradine leaves the dojo in the first place. Every episode he has flashbacks and remembers his time at the dojo learning all the Zen stuff and then he's out in these *Little House on the Prairie*–type studio sets, like it's the same place where they filmed Michael Landon in old-timey pioneer clothes. Carradine walks around the Midwest and he's just looking for trouble. The show makes no sense really in this way, but it's still something to watch, but I refrain from telling this short Japanese fella what I'm really thinking about and how I want to maim him because he made it known he's carrying a piece right in front of my girl.

Thugs, whether from Japan or wherever, I don't ever argue with them. I'm no thug and I have no shots to call like they do, so here I sit with this criminal in his Jeep Cherokee. The smell of the leather and the feeling of the air conditioner is a switch from the weather outside, but I can smell the little man's cologne and it's a foul. You'd never catch me wearing a fragrance that cheap.

"Mr. Benjamin, thanks so much for accommodating us."

"Yeah, sure," I say, looking out the window watching my girl stand there on the sidewalk holding her paper bags with string handles. I notice how she absentmindedly swings them around her waist back and forth with her arms like a little kid as we drive off.

"Let me get to the point, Mr. Benjamin."

"You can call me Ben," I tell him once more.

"Yes, Mr. Ben. My name is Tokyo Steve."

I want to laugh when he says this, but I don't.

"It has come to our attention that I must manage Mr. Jen Zen's assets in a manner that may not agree with you. You see, being from Japan like we are we have limited resources to conduct business when we are in town. We don't have access to institutions like we normally would in our own country."

"Like banks?" I say because I can see where this is going. Jen Zen obviously gambled away his cash when he shouldn't have. Gambling addictions. Funny those.

"Due to these unfortunate circumstances we must take back your winnings. In exchange for this transaction you will receive two airline tickets and accommodations at Jen Zen's island resort in Fiji. During your stay you will not want for anything. Room service to shopping expeditions, you will be fully compensated. We will also hold poker games there during your stay and you will need no money for a buy in and we will sponsor it with no worry of paying it back if there are losses. No money will come from your pocket during your stay, Mr. Ben. Do you understand our generous offer in compensation for this inconvenience to you?"

"Whatever." I remove the backpack from my shoulders and put it in the middle seat between us. "Jen Zen obviously needs it more than I do."

"Thank you, Mr. Ben," and Flash takes the bag, putting it at his feet on the car floor. "It's also come to our attention that you and your girlfriend have a child."

The hair on the back of my neck goes on end like a cold chill has hit just that one spot.

"Delivered to your address will be a series of gifts from Mr. Jen Zen. There will be gifts appropriate for your child's age. I think you will find the items selected enjoyable and satisfactory for your child."

This freaks me out that he knows where I live, but should I be surprised? All rich jerks, no matter which country they come from, are crooks through and through. I don't know who would've told this criminal where I live. I'm not listed in the phone book or the white pages. Did Joey-Nine tell him? I can't believe he would do that. It can't be him. I guess I'm paranoid. They had my phone number, so I guess it would be easy to look up my address. Thugs like Flash always got one up on me in the end, but even Jesus sat in front of the devil once and listened to what he had on offer. I imagine Jesus doesn't play poker much, but if he did, he'd just win all the time. Just ask any hardcore fundamental Christian type and they'd surely agree with me.

"It's not a problem," I say, ready to get out of the car now. "Tell Mr. Iotonka I accept his offer. A vacation sounds all right, honestly," and I think about the *Conde Nast* magazine sitting on the coffee table back home.

"Tell me, will ya, Tokyo Steve?" I ask because I'm curious. "What's the emergency Jen Zen needs this money for?"

"I am not at liberty to talk about Mr. Jen Zen's business. I'm sure you can understand my position."

"You got it." I shrug. "I gotta get back to my girl now, Stevie."

Mr. Tokyo Steve says something in Japanese to the driver. I look at the back of the neck of the big Japanese guy sitting up front. His thick, wrinkly, buzzcut neck reminds me of the wrinkles on the tough skin of a fat brown and white spotted cow in a pasture chewing cud.

We pull around the block and I hear the clicking sound of yellow lights as the driver puts them on again to stop. I turn to shake Mr. Tokyo Steve's hand and then tell the sumo wrestler up front I can let myself out. I exit the vehicle trying to imagine what Jen Zen needs the cash for. Does he owe some LA mobster money? Does he have to take one of his mistresses on a shopping spree in Beverly Hills like I did yesterday? I guess it's better that I'll never know. I'm sure it's safer for me not to.

I hear the window on the Jeep Cherokee go down behind me again and hear Stevie's stupid voice once more. "There's one more thing, Mr. Ben. We trust you won't mention our conversation to anyone. Upholding Mr. Jen Zen's reputation is of the upmost importance here in Little Tokyo as you can understand."

Tokyo Steve pats his breast pocket again and I just can't believe it. *The fucking prick!*

"I understand," I say.

Tokyo Steve smiles and it's creepy. "Goodbye, then, Mr. Ben."

I walk back to Amika, who's standing there waiting for me. I grab her by the waist and kiss her on the lips, letting her know everything's okay, and behind me I hear the Jeep Cherokee finally drive off.

"Your backpack's gone."

"I'll explain it to you later, babe." My hand is in my pocket and I realize I still have that roll of hundreds on me.

"Guess what? We're going on a trip to Fiji. A vacation."

"What?" She's elated by the idea.

"Yeah, we'll have to hire your mom again to babysit little Davey a while longer."

I think maybe I should tell her about the gifts for her kid, but realize I can do it later. My girl never asks me about the details of these weird people I meet at illegal games and I can appreciate that. Why would I want to explain to her how much scum there is out there? These greedy sore losers with guns?

I feel the difference of the heat change because the sun is setting and the sky is going from pink to purple and to a darker hue of blue in the sky. Tourists walk up and down the sidewalk having no idea about the backpack with the ninety-plus grand, the black Cherokee, and the Japanese criminals driving around town. They don't even know about the illegal poker game that happened in the building across the street this morning.

My girl's hair is getting frizzy because of how hot it is today. She's put her hair up in a scrunchie she bought at the shop earlier. I see the perspiration that's formed on her neck and I'm reminded of her humanity. She's carrying her bags full of makeup and some Hello Kitty toys she picked out for Little Davey.

I'm overpowered by a feeling of needing her. It has to be the gun in that guy's breast pocket that makes me feel this way. I don't like it, this helpless feeling where I control nothing. It's depressing. I could cry, right now, standing here on this busy street like some existential jerkoff. I could start asking questions about life and all the crappy contents of it because of my gambling, but instead I force myself to start thinking about something else.

"I love you, Amika."

"I love you, too," she says back. She looks at me and holds my hand tight and at least she's excited about this trip to Fiji. It's the little things and all that.

I start to pay attention to the Japanese village, which is full of people as the evening approaches. I breathe more. We pass a newsstand and I see the same headline I saw earlier about the Asian markets causing the Dow to fall over 500 points.

Is that why Iotonka needed the money?

Up ahead is a man selling ice cold water out of a granny cart. He's getting one-dollar bills for 12 oz. bottles of water from sweating tourists walking down the street. The granny cart is lined with black, plastic garbage bags and you can see the condensation forming out onto the sidewalk from the wet bottom.

"That's a good business," I say to Amika.

"No, it isn't." She giggles in reply.

Suddenly I'm struck with laughter, too, because I realize I know exactly what she means.

Letters in the Attic

Shana Scott

DANIEL OPENED THE DOOR TO THE ATTIC, TOOK A LONG LOOK AROUND THE dusty room, and groaned to himself. He didn't groan aloud, that would have been rude to his grandmother, who waited in her wheelchair at the bottom of the attic stairs, eyes still raw from days of crying, but he still loathed what would no doubt be several days breathing in the soot of fifty years' neglect, or at least ten, which was how long it had been since his grandparents could walk up or down stairs by themselves.

"What's up there?" his grandmother asked in a voice thickened by years of smoking. She'd quit a decade or more before when breathing got hard, but the damage lingered. "It's been so long, I can't remember it all."

He shoved his internal regret at having volunteered to help her pack up and donate much of his, now late, grandfather's things. He was on summer break from college and had moved into his grandparents' house to help care for his grandfather and save his mother the stress. A good deal considering he got room and board in the process. Without his grandfather, only his grandmother needed help, and right now he didn't have the heart to complain about the dust. She'd cried so much in the last week.

Daniel smiled down at her as he took out his cell phone. "Hang on a minute. I'll take some pictures so you can see."

"Oh, that's such a smart idea," she said, her gaze finally matching the brightness in her voice. "Guess that's why they sent you to college."

Daniel chuckled to himself. "Yes, Grandma."

He flicked the lights—nothing, he'd need to change the bulbs next time he came up here—and started taking pictures, flash on. There was so much stuff. If they'd received more from his grandfather's life insurance, Daniel would have suggested hiring a magic weaver to clean the place lickety-split, but even everyday spells cost too much for them at the moment. That left Daniel to sift through odd pieces of furniture, most missing a piece or two, half broken lamps or knickknacks, and so many boxes neatly labeled in his grandmother's handwriting.

Mama's winter clothes, beach supplies, Paul's (Daniel's uncle, the graphic designer) *grade school art projects, grandchildren's cards* (why keep cards?), *Daddy's WWII letters and papers* . . .

Daniel paused in his pictures at the last box. He knew his grandfather had served during World War II—he'd gotten buried in a national cemetery for it not four days ago—but that was all. He didn't know they'd kept anything from that time. As a history major, he allowed himself the chance to open this box.

His grandfather never talked about the war, even if asked. His grandmother said that it was painful for him to remember those times since he'd been more than a draftee. His grandfather signed up right out of high school, before the war began, and worked his way up the ranks. Having other soldiers' lives in his hands hadn't been hard, she said, until the war began and he lost more than he could remember the names of. He retired from the military after the war ended.

Daniel used the illumination from his phone to light inside the box. A few envelopes with official-looking seals on them, a medal he didn't recognize in a little box, and a bundle of letters all addressed to MaryAnn Lantham tied together in thin, frayed twine. The letters were smaller than paper today, square envelopes of half the normal size. His grandmother must have kept every scrap of paper she'd ever received in the mail. The box of cards suddenly made more sense.

Daniel grabbed the bundle and fingered through the envelopes to count how many there were, when a slip of paper—cleaner and undamaged compared to the war letters—fluttered to his feet. It had been between several letters. Daniel tucked the bundle under one arm before using his phone to find the errant paper.

Don't let him remember.

He stared at the cursive script, much steadier in youth but undoubtedly his grandmother's. Don't let him remember what? Now Daniel was doubly curious. He stuck the bundle in his pocket to ask his grandmother and finished taking pictures. He was headed back to the stairs when he heard his grandmother's wheezing cry. Daniel barreled down the stairs two at a time to find her couched over in her wheelchair weeping with a rosary in her hands.

"Grandma, are you okay?"

She dismissed him with a wave that didn't comfort him. "I'm sorry. I shouldn't still be . . . it's just, I was thinking about the last time I was up there . . . Sam had been with me and then . . ."

"It's okay. We can look at the pictures when you're feeling more up to it. Let's go have lunch." Daniel hugged his grandmother and spoke softly as he led her away from the attic to find her inhaler before making lunch, the letters forgotten until late that night when his pants made a thud as he undressed for bed.

Daniel fingered the letters again as he pulled them from the discarded pants. He'd originally thought his grandmother would enjoy talking about his grandfather, but after her reaction to Daniel going up to the attic, that no longer seemed a good idea. Seeing his grandfather's handwriting and talking about the war might only stress her more.

 Maybe if he only gave her a good letter, like a love letter, that would be all right. Surely in all these messages, one must talk about how much his grandfather loved and missed her. Then, if she asks to see the others, he could give them to her. Daniel nodded to himself, pleased with his plan, and snapped the aged twine with a quick tug not even strong enough to wrinkle the paper too much. He pulled the first letter from the pile and carefully unfolded it.

September 15, 1943

My Dearest MaryAnn,

God I miss you. Did I tell you that in my last letter? If I ever forget to say it, know it's true. I'm glad you're far away from this war, but I wish I was at your side now. I wish it more than you'll ever know.

We took Sicily. Those Egyptian spell-slingers know what they're doing. With their help we took the entire island in a day and pushed on to Italy. Guess Mussolini should have begged his kraut buddies for some better magic. Their protections were as good as paper against the Egyptians. It's a small foothold, but we're here. Not that we didn't pay for, and won't continue paying for it.

I lost so many, MaryAnn, and what's worse, I can barely remember their faces. These young boys die before I even know them. It gets harder every time they send me new recruits fresh from basic. And now I've got these Egyptian boys, too. Can't even ask their names without a translator. Until replacements come, the top brass combined my unit with an Egyptian company that didn't fare too much better so we can hold our position. I don't know how the krauts can make so much shit about race and nationality. When I look at my camp, they're all just children. They thought they'd play the soldier, and now they see what that really means.

It's sad how easy it is to pick out the ones who've been here longest. Most of those boys are in shock now, mourning their friends and wondering how they can be happy to have survived. Then you have the older men, they don't sit with the boys. Those boys haven't earned the right to sit with them yet. You have to survive—and keep surviving— otherwise it hurts too much to get to know them and watch them die over and over. I try not to be like that, but it's getting harder. When I do, I imagine you standing behind me, scolding me for not being polite. It helps—having you in my ear.

Strange thing is, some of the Egyptians sat with the old survivors, including this young, barely-out-of-the-cradle Egyptian boy. He was a translator, but no one really talked. They didn't need to. They knew each other by the look in their eyes. So why'd this kid sit with them? I went over and looked at him and realized he belonged there, too. What did that boy go through to be accepted by those old soldiers? I think it'd hurt my heart too much to know.

I'm sorry to burden you with this, but as their commanding officer, I can't talk to anyone under me. I have to be strong or I can't expect them to be, and right now, we all need to be strong.

Tell Paul I love him. I know he's not old enough to understand or remember me, but tell him anyway. You two are what I'm fighting for. You're what keeps me going.

Love,

Sam

Daniel set the letter down on the worn and faded quilt his grandmother bought decades ago and tried to hear the voice of his grandfather as a younger man, barely thirty if Uncle Paul was still an infant. Daniel knew of only one picture of him from back then, and it'd never seemed to be the same person as the weathered man Daniel had grown up calling Grandpa. He couldn't quite find the voice, either.

Instead Daniel let the voice of his favorite history professor fill in the gaps to paint a picture of the war during that letter. The US was still in its first year of active fighting after Japanese sorcerers had blown up Pearl Harbor and bombs burned half the Hawaiian Islands. Egypt joined only a few months before, after Italy attempted to take a foothold in Northern Africa. His professor, Dr. Barnhart, liked to say the stupidest thing that happened in the entire war was pissing off the Egyptians. If they'd have left Africa alone, it would have been years before the Allies got a strong hold on central Europe. Italy had a better navy, but Egypt had better magic.

Shaking himself out of his historic reverie, Daniel remembered what he'd been looking for before he'd gotten distracted by the details. A love letter. He wanted a love letter to cheer his grandmother up.

Daniel respectfully folded and filed the letter back into its envelope before moving on to the next.

September 30, 1943

My Dearest MaryAnn,

I love you. I know you probably haven't received my previous letter yet, we only got mail out a few days ago, but writing to you helps me. It reminds me that there's a whole world of people like you living lives not touched by this war. I imagine you reading to Paul or cooking dinner or getting dressed for bed in that nightgown that's a little too short, the one that makes me drop something just so you'll bend over to pick it up. The little daily things keep me going. I can't wait to be in bed with you the next time you wear that nightgown.

We haven't moved yet, but a few ships broke past the Egyptian blockade and that leaves us flanked by land and sea until they're destroyed. We've called in reinforcements, but most of our navy is tied up in the Pacific. We're hoping to get some British ships to join the Egyptians soon. Until then, we can't risk moving from shore in numbers.

We're lucky to have the commander of the Egyptian company. He's surprised me. They promoted him to take over from the previous commander who'd died while taking the coast. I thought for sure he wasn't going to have a clue how to handle it—he didn't seem ready for the command when I first met him—but his ideas are like he's been in war all his life. He understands the rhythm of the battle and can dance while I'm just here flailing to keep from getting killed. I trust my gut, but I'm not so prideful as to ignore sound advice when I hear it, and his advice is keeping casualties down.

Funny I can like a man I've never said two words to. He doesn't speak English and I don't speak Coptic. I know more about his translator than I do him, but then his translator feels more like one of us old soldiers than this commander does. If he wasn't so smart, I'd swear this was the man's first time in real battle. Goes to show I need to listen to your scolding voice more often and not judge people too quickly. Obviously I'm lost without you.

> *I need to go, but I'll write again, even if the mail doesn't go out.*
> *Love forever,*
> *Sam*

Daniel hurried to find the next letter, having forgotten his original goal and the fact he'd been getting ready for bed in favor of the fascination unfolding on yellowed, creased paper. He never knew his grandfather had been smack in the middle of the Sicilian invasion force. Taking the Italian coast gave the Allied powers a foothold into Europe that cut years off the war, and here was a firsthand account. The history major in Daniel couldn't resist.

In his effort to retrieve the next letter, Daniel's hand brushed the scrap of paper that had been with the bundle, and he paused long enough to wonder again why his grandmother didn't want his grandfather to remember this. It must have been terrible, but enough to warrant a note and the hiding of letters? Daniel read on.

October 13, 1943

My Dearest MaryAnn,

If I ever forget to begin my letter by telling you how much I miss you and love you and want to be with you, then be sure to yell at me in your reply, but know it's true anyway and you're always in my thoughts. You are what keeps my heart beating. You and Paul.

I wish I could just send a normal love letter, writing bad poetry and comparing your eyes to the crystal blue waters of the Italian coast. The water isn't very clear or blue right now, though, and I respect you too much to send lies even in the form of bad poetry. And, besides, I need to feel like you're talking to me to help me work through something that's bugging me. You always had a knack for making my problems seem simpler, so, if you don't mind, not that you can really stop me, (something else you should be used to) I'm going to lay out what's happening and pretend you're here helping me through it. When you get this, send me back your thoughts, in case I don't do your voice in my head the justice you deserve.

Something isn't right with the commander I told you about. The Egyptian one. He—he doesn't make sense. Nothing about him makes sense. He offers field strategies and tactics that have saved more lives than I could ever have on my own. His mind is everything a seasoned veteran should have, and yet, he's not a seasoned veteran. He's not even a good leader to his own men.

An Italian company attacked from the north, and while we followed his plan to push them back and take some ground at the same time—a good plan—he struggled to remember where to send his men or when to begin the artillery barrage. It's as if he's two people: one who's calm, smart, and calculating, and the other a frantic man given leadership before he was ready.

At first, I thought it was just a matter of nerves. That when he wasn't being shot at, he could collect himself enough to think, but then under fire he gets flustered. But it's not just that. I watched him last time we talked. I may not understand the language, but body language isn't that different, and he doesn't look like someone who knows what he's doing. No confidence, no self-assurance. He looks at me like a man looking for answers, not one offering them.

Now, if I know you, you'd tell me that if I can't figure out the answer to the question, then maybe that question isn't the right one to be asking. And you'd be right, as you usually are. How can a man be so smart and inept at the same time? If that's the wrong question, what would the right one be? Someone has to think up these strategies, and if it's not the Egyptian commander, who is it? When we talk it's just me and him and—the translator.

It couldn't be. He's just a kid. Old as he seems sometimes, he can't be more than nineteen.

Could it really?

I need to think on this. I hope you have a better answer in your letter than your voice in my head.

With all my love,

Sam

Daniel let out a breath and headed for the next letter. He never imagined his grandfather as anything but the retired old man who didn't like to talk about serious matters and who in his last few years had forgot more than he remembered. Yet these letters made him seem larger than life—a man who people depended on to hold the line, to fight a war. What was it he wasn't supposed to remember?

October 17, 1943

My Dearest MaryAnn,

I love you. I miss you. I wish I could have been there for Paul's first step. He's going to have you on the run from now on. That's how quickly your letters are getting through, if you were wondering. You probably haven't even received my last letter yet.

Even so, things have developed since then, and I'm not certain what to do about it. I sent for another translator and had him listen, covertly, to our conversation. I'd hoped he'd confirm that my suspicions were unfounded, and the Egyptian commander was just a nervous genius. I wasn't that lucky, and now the situation is complicated.

It was the translator, Khamun Aten. The second translator said that every time Khamun told me the Egyptian commander had a plan, he would then tell his commander that I had the plan and repeat the same idea to both of us. That means this barely-more-than-a-boy translator has been keeping all of us alive for the last month by lying to everyone and the only explanation I can come up with is Khamun isn't what he seems. I think he might be one of them supernatural folk.

I know our troops segregate out supernaturals from the regulars, but the Egyptians don't. If they allow them in, then why would he be hiding out as a translator? Why not let everyone know so he can be more helpful? And what is he? It doesn't make any sense. The only way I'm going to get answers to my questions is to confront him, but if he is another kind of creature, then I've got no idea what he'll do.

I wish you were here to tell me what an idiot I am. That this boy, if he is a boy, has done nothing but help us and I should trust that no matter what he is. See, even in my head you're smarter than me.

Stay safe and know I love you,
Sam.

Daniel completely forgot his mission for a love letter as the story his grandfather wrote unfolded with each folded paper. War, supernaturals, and subterfuge. This was the best war story he'd ever heard, and neither of his grandparents had ever said a word about it.

October 24, 1943

My Dearest MaryAnn,
I love you and Paul. I miss you like I miss a home-cooked meal or a good night's sleep. I miss home. When this war is over, I intend to take you and Paul away for a week to a quiet place where we can be together.

I finally received your answer to my question about the Egyptian commander. It's good to know the voice in my head matches you so well, right down to your warning not to jump to conclusions if it turned out to be the translator. You'd be a force to be reckoned with if you were over here, but I'm glad you're nowhere near this hell.

I did talk to Khamun—with an open mind like you wanted. When I told him I knew he was lying, that he was the one coming up with the strategies we've been using, and that I thought he was more than human, the look on his face was so old. He aged a thousand years in a moment, in a breath. Or a sigh, as it was. It was wrong, that ancient expression on so young a face. But then he smiled and suddenly he was this boy again.

He wouldn't tell me what he is, but he did say he wasn't human, and this was far from the first war he'd been in. His goal is to keep Egypt from being invaded, and holding the Italian coast, and thus the Mediterranean, is the best way to do that. When I asked him why he wasn't using all his knowledge to help end this war, his answer frightened me. "The old kings of Egypt rode into battle with their armies. They didn't sit at desks looking at maps." I don't know if he was just making a point or if he is, in fact, ancient enough to be an old king of Egypt. I don't want to know.

But he is smart. Now that I know he's not human, he's teaching me more than I could imagine. There's not a captain or colonel I've met smarter than him. Generals probably could learn a few things, too. Assuming I survive this war with any will to keep my commission, and I can't promise that, with the things he's teaching me, I could definitely move up the ranks. You were right not to judge him for lying. He's a good guy, and with him I have a better chance of making it home to you. That's all that matters to me.

Forever yours,

Sam

p.s. I'm going to invite Khamun to come visit when the war's over. I think you'll like him.

A thousand questions ran through Daniel's head and the letters offered few answers. "Give me some details, Grandpa."

What was Khamun? What could he do? Could he turn into something? Was he immortal? Daniel heard some supernaturals lived a long time, but those were usually beasts. What kind of human-seeming creature could seem "ancient" as his grandfather described? What did Khamun teach him? Military? Science?

Daniel scrambled to find the next letter hoping for something more than vague descriptions.

November 4, 1943

My Dearest MaryAnn,

I swear I'm going to write you a damn love letter this time. It's going to be sappy, and lovey-dovey, and a hundred different forms of mushy sweetness. You better make a dentist appointment for this one. There'll be no talk of the war or any troubles or anything besides me telling you all that you mean to me. I promise, this time it's going to happen.

Khamun and I were talking—we've been talking a lot. Never thought I'd find a friend like him out here. But I'm not getting into that. This is your love letter. Anyway, he doesn't talk a lot about his past, but I told him all about you. About the way you snort just a little when you laugh too hard and then get embarrassed and snort even louder. About the way your nose crinkled up for hours when you were figuring out how to stretch the budget enough for us to buy the house. How much I miss arguing with you, because you demand me to be a better man, and it's my privilege to live up to who you see when you look at me.

When I finished getting thoroughly homesick, Khamun told me I should write to you and tell you all that. He told me that he loved a long time ago, and still loves to this day. And when he said "long" there was a meaning behind that word that no dictionary could capture. He said he wished he could have gone back and told himself when he first met her to not take a day for granted, to not wait so long to tell her how much he loved her, because once she was gone he felt like a lifetime with her hadn't been enough. So I shouldn't wait a single day, or a single letter, to tell you that without you in my life, I'd be lost.

Everything I do is to make sure you have the best life I can give you, the life you deserve. If I were to lose you—this brilliant, stubborn, kind, loving, sometimes impatient, funny because your jokes aren't really funny at all, beautiful, strong, fearless, and utterly amazing woman—I would have nothing left to fight for. And then the voice in my head that's you would tell me I was an idiot, and I better survive and get back to raise our son. And, once again, you'd be right.

I love you. I will always love you. I will love you to the day I die, and I hope that's a long time from now with you by my side.
Forever yours,
Sam

Daniel blew out all the air in his lungs, eyes wide as he re-read the letter. It wasn't Shakespearean poetry or the most eloquent hand a novelist could dream up, but Daniel could feel his grandfather's desperate need to convey feelings that had become rote to Daniel as he read the beginning to all these letters. To his grandfather those weren't sentimental feelings he was required to say because it was a letter to his wife. To him, they were the reason he kept going when the world around him went to hell.

Daniel reverently folded the letter, put it back into its envelope, and set it aside from the rest of the bundle. That was a letter his grandmother needed to see. It would make her happy to remember that his grandfather got his wish in the end.

It almost felt disrespectful to continue reading after that letter, but after a few minutes of pretending to get ready for bed again, curiosity won out and Daniel sat down to read what happened next. There was still the question of what his grandfather wasn't supposed to remember.

A knot turned his stomach to stone and made each breath heavy. Splotches darkened the paper and spread the ink in watery trails, as if rain—or tears—splashed while writing.

November 16, 1943

My Dearest MaryAnn,
I love you. Knowing you're safe seems to be the only kind thought I can bring to mind these last few days.
We're not in the best place now, MaryAnn. I wish I could tell you I was safe and we've got the Italians on the run, but if things go bad, I

don't want the last words I write to you to be a lie. Khamun and I are trying to find a way out of this mess, but even with all the knowledge Khamun has, I'm not sure we have the manpower or the resources to hold our line, and we definitely don't have the ships to evacuate us.

Even Khamun's worried. I can tell. He's been watching the men, like a general surveying troops when he knows his orders will get them killed. Or a soldier leaving for home and knowing he probably wouldn't see any of his friends again. I think he'll survive whatever comes, even if we don't.

If he does and I don't, I've asked him to find you to return my wedding ring and to come back when Paul's old enough to tell him about the man I was during the war. You'll have him idolizing me as a hero, but he deserves to the know the good and the bad, when he's old enough to understand. I want to be a real person to him, not just memories clouded by grief. Please don't hate Khamun for surviving. It's not his fault he's more than human.

Be strong. Raise Paul to be as amazing a person as you. Tell him I wish I could have been there for him growing up, and I'll be looking down from wherever I am. Always.

Yours to the end,

Sam

The letter crinkled as Daniel wiped at his face with the back of his hand. What was it like to write a letter like that? Daniel couldn't fathom the resolve his grandfather needed to write to his wife that it was probably going to be the last letter she ever received from him. Knowing that he survived the war did nothing to mitigate the ache that kept Daniel's jaw tight to hold in the sob threatening to break free. He blew his nose and returned the letter to the pile. There was only one left, and its envelope was smudged with rusty brown fingerprints that Daniel was pretty sure wasn't rust.

Inside, the same reddish-brown splotches marred the paper, but it was the frantic scrawled handwriting that caught Daniel's eyes. All the letters previously had been clean and fairly easy to read, but the writing on this one slanted and twisted like the writer couldn't keep the paper straight in his rush to get the words down. Whatever his grandmother didn't want his grandfather to remember was probably in this letter.

N 18 1943

MaryAnn. I need to get this down before he gets back and makes me forget. I need to remember. Someone needs to remember. It shouldn't be his burden alone. I asked him. He's doing it for me, to save us, but he's going to make me forget and I need to remember. I need [unintelligible scribbles] made me forget before. It's the only explanation how I didn't notice he never went out in daylight. It's a war! I would have not noticed! He had've made me forget. I need a record to make me remember. Show this to me when I get home. Don't let me forget!

It started when the Italian navy broke the Egyptian blockade and their army pushed from the north. We weren't the only ones pinned, but we didn't have enough people to hold them off. No magic users, nothing. Then they landed on the coast and there was nothing to do. Half the company, mine and the Egyptian's, was already wounded or dead. In all the chaos I couldn't find Khamun. What was left of us ended up trapped in an old building, half demolished by magic and bombs. We could hear the machine gun firing. It was only a matter of time.

Then I finally saw Khamun. His uniform wasn't as filthy as ours were and he had a dark blanket draped down from his head. I realized then that he hadn't been in the fight at all. It didn't make sense. I asked him where he'd been while we were dying. He said he had to wait until the bombs gave him enough cover from the sun to move. He couldn't be in the sun! All this time I never noticed never remembered I'd only ever talked to him inside a tent or at night. He must've done something to make me forget.

I asked him to save us. I begged him, if he was really a supernatural, if he really had powers, to please help. I didn't want to die that way. I didn't want to leave you alone. I wanted to see my son once before I died. I told him all that and the expression on his face [blood and tears smeared the next few words that might have been "sorrow" and "endless"] I begged him to let me tell you one more time how much I loved you.

He said he could help, but people couldn't see what he was. He said that if people knew creatures like him existed, no supernatural would ever be safe again and a war would break out between humans and supernaturals that would make this one seem like a scuffle between children. If he went out there to save us, he wouldn't just push them back, he'd have to slaughter anyone who saw him, because under sunlight he can't hide what he is. I was so terrified then, I didn't realize what he was saying. I couldn't understand the impact of what he meant. I didn't see the pain he was in. I get it now. I finally understand why he was a translator and not openly a supernatural. Not to hide what he is, not entirely. He was a translator so he didn't have to become the monster inside him. He didn't want to slaughter anyone, not even the enemy. He's done it before. I can see it, now that I'm thinking back. He didn't want to kill.

But at that moment I just wanted to be able to go home to you. I didn't want to die. So I begged him again.

He's a good man. He's my friend. And he was willing to protect me—protect us. So he became the monster to save me. He did something to the men, made them calm. You can't make someone who's terrified they're about to die turn off the adrenaline. But he did. The men all got quiet and turned away from the few windows, not that we were close to them. They all huddled together with their eyes to the wall, so he wouldn't have to kill them too. He was about to do it to me, I could tell. I told him, it's my fault he's doing this and I needed to witness it. I swore I would never tell. He was my friend and he was saving my life.

Khamun gave me the most horribly sad smile and told me when it was over, I wouldn't want to remember. He was wrong. I need to remember what he sacrificed for me. But he's going to take it, just like before. He won't want me to remember what happened.

Khamun took one of the men aside from the rest, not one of the wounded, and bit into his wrist with fangs he'd never had before. His eyes turned red as the devil and he drank the blood greedily. Even with cover he'd hurt himself going out in daylight. He said he'd need strength if he was going to make it to the enemy. The one he drank from didn't seem hurt, just sat down quietly and closed his eyes. Then Khamun leapt out of the window near us—three stories up—and the screaming started.

At first the gunfire kept me from getting close to the window, but soon no one was firing at us anymore. When I looked out, the whole area was in chaos. Not the chaos of battle. It was like a beehive crashed open but instead of swarming the one who attacked them, all the bees were flying away as fast as they could only to get snatched right out of the air and have their wings ripped off. Only it wasn't wings. Sometimes it was arms. Sometimes it was heads. And Khamun guzzled down their blood as fast as he killed. He had to. Whenever the sunlight touched him, his skin and flesh burned away down to the bone. I swear once his face was nothing but a skull held together by flaming tendons. He bit into a man's neck, tipping him over his head like a glass he wanted to get the last drink from, and as the blood filled him, muscles and skin regrew only to turn black under the sun again.

The slaughter wasn't just because he couldn't let anyone know what he was. In order to save us, he had to kill them all or he'd burn to ash under the sun. This is my fault. I begged him to become this. I begged him to be a monster so I could see you again. So I need to remember. I need to know the sin I committed on a good man to save myself.

There aren't many screams now. I need to hurry and get this tucked away so I'll send it to you and you can give it to me.

I need to remember.

Daniel folded the letter back up and sat staring at his hands in his lap for nearly a half hour. He didn't even know what shocked him more: that what his grandfather described happened, that his grandfather apparently didn't remember it, or that the only creature

Daniel could imagine from the letter was a vampire, and vampires didn't exist. Sorcerers and supernaturals all said there was no such thing as the undead. Stories of such were misidentifications of other creatures or tricks of animation magic. There were no creatures that lurked in the darkness and drank innocent humans' blood.

But wouldn't that be a secret a real vampire would kill to keep? Wouldn't humans be terrified to know they were real?

Yes, that was definitely the one that shocked him—scared him— the most.

Sleep didn't come easy to Daniel that night. When it finally claimed him, dreams of blood-red eyes flashing in the darkness of a battlefield kept him running all night. He didn't show the letters to his grandmother the next morning, not even the love letter that he'd first searched for. He didn't know what she'd say, or if she even remembered anymore. If age had taken the memories away, he didn't want to be the one to bring them back to the surface, not so close to his grandfather's death.

While he cleaned up from supper, his grandmother pushed out her chair and turned to Daniel. "I'd like to go visit the grave site. Will you drive me?" she asked in a voice thick with sorrow and longing.

"Now?" Daniel glanced out the window. The day had been as dreary as a day could be and still be considered daytime, and that little light that made the clouds glow gray was already slipping lower on the horizon. It'd be dark in less than an hour, and he was pretty sure the cemetery hours ended at sundown.

"Yes," she said, as if she didn't notice his hesitation or the dim light coming in from the kitchen window.

Before reading those letters, Daniel would have put her off until the next day, not wanting to be bothered should the gates be closed when they arrived. Now he didn't just see the little old lady who taught him to cook and used to make costumes for him every Halloween. Now she was also MaryAnn, a woman his grandfather had loved and trusted and depended on, a woman who'd been smart enough to figure out all the same things his grandfather had without ever meeting the players. A woman who hadn't wanted to burden his grandfather again with memories of monsters who used to be friends.

Now, he respected his grandmother in a way he realized he hadn't before. She might need his help, but she wasn't a child to be told what to do. If she wanted to go to the grave right now, he'd take her.

It took nearly fifteen minutes for his grandmother to get ready to leave and another fifteen to drive to the cemetery, which left the already morose sky an ugly gray mess that threatened a stormy night ahead. The gates were open, though, so Daniel made his way down the curving road that cut through a sea of trimmed green grass and white marble headstones toward an area where the grass wasn't all grown in yet and small plaques in the packed earth marked the place where a headstone would later rest. He was rather proud he didn't once look at his map this time. The path had become familiar over the last few weeks.

Surprisingly he had to park a little behind where he normally did because another car blocked his preferred spot—a bright yellow SUV with windows tinted so dark Daniel couldn't see the seats inside. The plates were generic and bore the logo of a rental car company, though it wasn't one he recognized. Its occupant was visible though, standing among the newer graves—standing, Daniel realized, in front of his grandfather's grave.

He wasn't a large man, but the angle and growing darkness disguised his features from Daniel's roadside vantage. The man glanced back at the sound of the car door opening and quietly moved down the row a few graves, his eyes on the markers as if searching for a specific person among the sea of dead.

"Guess he was just checking out the new arrivals," Daniel murmured to himself as he helped his grandmother out of the car.

"What?" she asked, leaning heavily on her walker to move over the soft ground. Daniel stayed close behind. She could only go short distances without the wheelchair.

"The man, he was standing by Grandpa's grave when we got here. I said I suppose he was just checking out the new names."

His grandmother looked up, noticing the man for the first time—he was four graves down with his head bowed in respect. Now that they were closer, more of the man was visible, and Daniel was shocked by how young he was. The man couldn't have been more than twenty-one, if that even. Young people don't often go cemetery walking. What little of his skin that showed, which wasn't much, was a deep olive tan that would have looked more at home on some sunny beach in the Mediterranean, though his nose and jaw made the overall feeling more Middle Eastern than European.

Aside from his face, the man was covered from head to toe in layers, which made Daniel hot just looking at him. The humidity alone had Daniel sweating despite the fading light and cloud cover easing the summer heat some. A long brown trench coat covered an expensive blue button-down shirt and black slacks hanging over thick military-style boots. He even wore sleek, black-fingered gloves that both hid and displayed his long, lean hands. The man managed to pull off the neat but practical outfit, until he got to the oversized Stetson hat that nearly swamped his head, fell back over his neck, and turned the whole ensemble into a child playing dressup in his father's closet.

His grandmother watched the man with intense concentration, as if searching for something she recognized in his face, though Daniel was certain he at least had never met this man. He couldn't think of anyone his grandmother mentioned that might garner such attention, and it had to be recently if she'd met him, as young as he was. Despite the man's obvious attempt to ignore them both and focus on the grave, Daniel's grandmother walked herself right up to him against Daniel's hushed protest. When the man made no move to acknowledge her, she tapped on his arm.

The man politely turned to face her. "May I help you?" He didn't have any accent, but something in the cadence of his words made Daniel think that English wasn't the man's native language.

"I think I know you," she replied, still searching his eyes for . . . something.

The man offered a smile that one would when a strange old lady randomly comes up to you and claims to know who you are. "I don't believe we've met, ma'am."

"I didn't say we've met. I said I think I know you. I think your name is Khamun Aten. Is it?"

Daniel froze, which was better than revealing his shock with a gaping mouth and bulging eyes. The man was young. Middle Eastern features . . . which could include Egypt. He was covered from head to toe, like he didn't want any light touching his skin. Not that there was much light. Between the late hour and the cloud cover, it was quite dim. It couldn't possibly be him, though, could it?

The man didn't look any more prepared for the question. He shifted uncomfortably on one foot and patted his hat farther down on his head. "Where did you hear that name?"

"Sam wrote letters to me during the war," she said, revealing age had done nothing to steal her mind from her. "He'd tell me all his problems and ask for help figuring them out. He knew my replies would never make it back in time to do much, but it comforted him to write. He told me all about his supernatural translator who had eyes that seemed ancient, the Bible sense of ancient."

For a long moment the man stared at her as if he had no idea what she was talking about, then a bright smile that made his face five years younger blossomed along with a wry laugh. "You must be MaryAnn. Sam always said you were smarter than him. I guess I should've known if he wrote home, you'd figure it out. I'm sorry to hear he's gone. He was a good man."

"So are you." As she talked, his grandmother opened her purse and rifled around until she found her wallet. "He wrote to me of that night you saved him, what you had to become to do that. He regretted asking you to become a monster so he could live and come home to me, and he was afraid you'd make him forget everything, which you did. Thank you for that. He had enough to feel guilty about because of that war. It was better he didn't remember that. But I wished you'd let him remember you. When he came home, he didn't even know your name. That made me sad. You were a good friend to him."

The joyful expression faded quickly from Khamun's face. "I'm sorry you had to learn of that day. No one should need to remember that."

"Hogwash," his grandmother said with all the motherly scolding she could manage. "Sam wanted someone to remember what you sacrificed for them. And since he had enough demons on his mind, I gladly remember for him." She opened her wallet and pulled a folded piece of paper, yellow with time, from the main flap behind a five-dollar bill and held it out to Khamun. "I wrote this letter to you the day my Sam arrived home. I've carried it every day since then in case I ever saw you. You need to know what I felt that day. You need to know how grateful I am that you were willing to do things you hated to save my husband. He came home because of you, and for that I have thanked God for you every day in my prayers. And I really hope you don't make me forget that, because it's brought me great comfort that men like you exist."

With a reverence that Daniel didn't think anyone born in the last two hundred years could convey in a single motion, Khamun collected the paper between his palms and closed his eyes as if in prayer. He didn't read it, but enough had been said.

"Thank you," Khamun said, his voice barely more than a whisper. A melancholy smile crossed his face and Daniel wasn't sure if he should smile back or start crying at the sorrow it conveyed. "I saved him, because the way he described you sounded so much like my wife I couldn't bear to let you cry if I could stop it. I was right. You're just like my Riah. Knowing you had a lifetime of happiness, eases my heart. The last thing I'd do is take away anything that gives you comfort, even if the memory isn't a good one."

Like she was greeting an old friend, Daniel's grandmother pulled Khamun into a deep, warm hug that had Daniel blinking back tears. What if he hadn't read those letters and learned to see her in a different light? He might not have brought her here so late in the day. That would have denied her—and Khamun—a meeting seventy years in the waiting. Maybe fate, destiny, or God was watching out for them to make sure they didn't miss this chance.

His grandmother wiped away the tears she didn't hide and waved Daniel forward. "Mr. Aten, I'd like you to meet my grandson, Daniel. He wouldn't have been born if not for you. His mother was born two years after Sam came home. Daniel, this here is Khamun Aten. He's an old war buddy of your grandfather's, for all he looks nineteen."

"It's a pleasure to meet you," Daniel said, and he hoped the awe and trepidation shaking his voice was attributed to Khamun's age and not the fact Daniel also knew what happened that day in the war.

"Daniel is in college now. He's studying history. I don't know what part or what he's going to do with it, but he's studying it."

"*Grandma.*" This time the exasperation was real. "I'm still deciding what to do."

Khamun laughed a big booming laugh that didn't fit his lean frame. "I know a bit of history. There's a lot to learn. Ever consider Egyptology?"

Daniel was taken aback. He blinked a couple of times before replying. "You mean ancient Egypt and tombs and stuff? I thought that was archeology."

"Only if you want to open the tombs, and there's far too much red tape to do that these days. But there's still plenty of history there they haven't uncovered yet."

Daniel had a sinking feeling that Khamun was talking from experience, and wasn't that terrifying to imagine.

"If you decide you'd like to study it, contact Professor Moeshe Hanif at the museum in Cairo and mention my name. He'll put you on the right path. You might even see a few familiar faces." Khamun winked.

"Thank you, sir," Daniel said, involuntarily adding the honorific despite Khamun's appearance. He definitely wasn't Daniel's age.

His grandmother took Khamun's hand. "Why don't you come home with us? I'd love to show you pictures of the family and tell you about Sam."

Khamun shook his dark head, darker now that the last bit of illumination had faded into twilight. "I thank you for the offer, but I came to pay my respects and you've already given me a gift I shall cherish for years to come. Be well, MaryAnn."

He kissed her hand and bowed his head to her in respect before slipping away to drive into the darkness. Daniel took his grandmother's arm and they stood together at his grandfather's grave not needing to say a word.

When they finally returned the car, Daniel smiled to his grandmother. "I found some letters in the attic I think you'll want back."

Murder at Black Beck

Charles W. Warren

AMOS VAISEY WAS ABOUT HALFWAY DOWN THE MOUNTAIN WHEN A GUST OF wind thumped his shoulder and pulled aside the curtain of snow and mist in front of him. Far below he glimpsed Black Beck Hut and the dark ribbon of the stream beside it. Nearer, much nearer, he saw something lying on the path—before the wind dropped and the snow filled his line of sight again.

A BRIGHT ARC OF blood had leapt from the woman's throat across the whiteness. She was lying on her back, her feet pointing up the path and a great gaping tear in her neck. Vaisey had seen many such things in the trenches and in his work since then, but something about this prostrate soul out here in one of the remotest spots in England brought his quick mind to a screeching halt. He needed a cigarette, but his injured lungs had denied him that refuge for years.

He looked around him before he bent down beside the body. There was nothing to be done for her; she'd been here about an hour judging by the snow on her heavy brown coat and woolen gloves. It was her complexion that struck Vaisey and her eyes of deepest brown that stared up into the gray sky. She must be from the Near East, British Palestine perhaps. What on earth was she doing up here?

There was a bulge in one of the coat's waist pockets. He pulled a purse out and opened it. A few coins and ten-shilling notes, but no clue to who she was. He was about to replace the wallet when he noticed a folded paper among the banknotes. It was an invitation to a lecture by the American prohibitionist William Eugene Johnson in Glasgow. Vaisey knew a little about him . . . not a popular fellow with the brewing industry.

He replaced the purse and stood up. Her steps in the snow up the hill were clear enough for now but fast disappearing. It was as if she had simply walked into whoever had killed her. A second set of prints, again small, led down the hill but away from the path.

He circled the spot and behind a low bank of rock found a patch of trodden grass. Steps led from it to the dead woman. Perhaps the killer had waited here . . . and maybe for quite some time because any footprints to the spot had disappeared.

Vaisey returned to the path. He needed to get down the hill and call the police right away. Below him he glimpsed Black Beck Hut again. He was surprised to see a whisper of smoke arise from the trees next to it, lingering for a moment before it was snatched away by the wind.

His LUNGS, SCOURED BY mustard gas eight years ago, were burning by the time he reached the wooden door of the hut and pushed it open. For a moment, his snow-scalded eyes could see nothing but the glow of a lamp and a small fire struggling in a grate on the other side of the room.

"Shut the bloody door." Vaisey made out a tall, heavily built man sitting by a paraffin lamp.

There was a movement next to him and from the corner of his eye, he saw a woman stand up and push the door shut. She left behind a scent of whisky and damp wool as she sat back down.

"I need the phone, right away."

"There's no phone here," said the woman. She spoke precisely, a slight Cumbrian accent smoothing the edge off her cut-glass tones.

"This is the Lake District, not bloody Mayfair, you know," grunted the seated man. An empty pipe between his teeth bobbed up and down as he spoke.

Vaisey ignored him. "There's a woman's body out on the hills. We need to contact the police."

"What are you talking about?" The rude fellow stood up and Vaisey could see him clearly now. He must have been at least six foot four and about forty years of age. He had a full beard and was wearing expensive tweeds. Ex-military no doubt.

"There's a dead woman on the path . . ."

A third figure joined them from behind a rough wooden serving counter at one end of the little room. He was wearing an apron. "Are you Captain Amos Vaisey? I have a booking for a Captain Vaisey for tonight and tomorrow. Fine weather you picked for your vacation, sir."

"Please, there's a dead woman on the path. We urgently need to get in touch with the police."

"Captain Vaisey?" The first man pulled the empty pipe from his mouth. "The Captain Vaisey? Military Cross at Ypres . . . then Scotland Yard's finest detective and now a private investigator. Can't open the *Sketch* without reading about him. I salute you, sir. Major James Morris, ex–North Norfolks, also enjoying an ill-timed stroll in our wonderful Lakeland."

Morris reached Vaisey and shook his hand. "Delighted," said Vaisey, too preoccupied to sound anything like it. "If there's no phone, I need you or this gentleman," he turned to the man in the apron "to come with me back up the hill. There's a dead body up there."

"My name is Richards. I run this hostel. This is terrible." He brushed a lump of heavily oiled red hair away from his face.

"I'll come," said the woman. "I know these parts better than anyone."

"Bit chilly for a woman," said Morris.

"She's right, she does, and she's no ordinary woman," said the hostel manager. There was a hint of reprimand in his tone, his baby pink cheeks flushing.

"I'll come." Morris picked up his coat. "Sherlock here can lead the way."

Vaisey was glad to get out of the smoky hut; it wasn't doing his lungs much good in there. Outside the snow had ceased.

THE WOMAN CAST AN appraising look at Vaisey as they retraced his steps up the hill. Now that he was out of the gloomy hut, Vaisey could see that she was tall, and about thirty. Her face had something of the unyielding beauty of all those classical statues in the V&A Museum. There was a rugged firmness about her body and yet her gestures came with the elegance and assurance of wealth.

She smiled. "Convenient you should turn up when some poor soul has had their throat cut. Are you sure you have nothing to do with this?"

"I turn up at many places where no one has been murdered. We haven't been introduced."

She extended her hand and Vaisey was surprised to see she wasn't wearing any mittens, in spite of her long woolen coat and fox fur hat. "Emilia Greaves. My family own most of the pubs and hotels in the county. Kendal to Keswick."

He held her pale, ringless fingers for a second. "No walking holiday for you then."

"I love being out on these fells, even in this weather. My fiancé and I would walk for miles around here before the war . . . now I just enjoy the beauty of this place on my own."

"I'm sorry," said Vaisey.

"Oh, he came back from the war. Just not for me."

MORRIS STARED AT THE body. "Poor thing," he finally said.

"I know her," said Miss Greaves. "This is Adela Houghton. Her husband farms over in the next valley. He fought in Palestine with TE Lawrence. She came back with him and they married last year."

"Must have caused quite a hoo-ha bringing an Arab girl back to a place like this," said Morris. He was packing his pipe with tobacco.

"It did. We should cover her up." Miss Greaves' voice was so flat, she may as well have been talking about a sheep carcass. "The crows will take her eyes and there are weasels and foxes up here."

"I have a blanket in my rucksack." Vaisey ran a damp mitten across his bare head. Another wartime keepsake. By the time he came out of the hospital after that gas attack all his hair had fallen out, and the ringing in his ears from all the bombardments he had endured was permanent.

He turned to Miss Greaves. "Mrs. Houghton's husband, was he your former fiancé?"

"He was." Miss Greaves took his blanket and lay it over the body.

Morris stamped his feet. "It's perishing cold up here. We should save the chitchat for back at the hut. You, Vaisey, you should put your cap back on."

Vaisey returned to the spot where he believed the killer had waited. He looked at the ground and at the surface of the waist-high shelf of rock in front of him. Tiny puddles of a brown liquid sat in a small patch of the pockmarked stone. He rubbed a finger in it and put it to his nose. Whisky.

Miss Greaves cried out and he looked up. A figure in a long great coat was running out of the mist toward them.

"Oh my God," shouted the newcomer, flinging himself down by the body and pulling away the blanket. His cry of agony ended in a broken dry sob. "Adela, Adela . . ."

Mr. Houghton? wondered Vaisey.

Tears sat on a broad handsome face reddened by wind and weather as the bewildered farmer looked up at the three of them. Tufts of red hair peeped out from beneath his cap. "One of you . . ." he started but saw Vaisey and fell silent.

Miss Greaves dropped to her knees beside him and laid an arm across his shoulder. "My poor dear Jonathan, I'm so sorry."

THE THREE MEN CARRIED the body down the hill. Richards suggested they put Mrs. Houghton in a woodshed that stood next to the accommodation hut and was overshadowed by a stand of conifers. Vaisey noticed footprints in the snow that led into the trees from the shed.

Inside, they laid her on a crude wooden table, next to stacks of logs, a heap of pale kindling, and an axe, its head sunk into a broad piece of oak. There was something odd about the shape of the shed, but Vaisey could not put a finger on what it was.

Once back inside the hut, they sat before the fire, Houghton's grief filling the little room. Miss Greaves produced a whisky flask, but Houghton shook his head. Richards brought them all tea, and piled logs into the flames. On the wall above the fire hung an ancient shotgun, with open hammers on each barrel like some old musket. Morris lit his pipe.

"Someone must go to the police," said Vaisey.

"Who put you in charge?" Richards took a pull of Miss Greaves' whisky. "I'm the manager here."

"Be quiet, Anthony." It was the farmer. Vaisey was surprised he used Richards' first name.

"Well, I'm not going," said Richards. "It's snowing again, so why don't we just wait until the weather clears. Our foreign friend in the woodshed will keep."

Houghton, in spite of his grief, raised his head and stared at the little manager.

"I could go," said Miss Greaves.

Vaisey answered the manager first. "There's a killer somewhere out there, that's why it can't wait. That's also why Miss Greaves should stay here. Neither Morris nor I am familiar with this territory so, Mr. Houghton, I'm sorry to press you at a time like this . . ."

"I'll go," said the farmer.

"You should take this." Vaisey fished in his backpack and offered Houghton his old army revolver.

Houghton's eyes flicked to Miss Greaves and back to Vaisey. "I've not touched one of those things since 1918 and I'm not about to start now."

Vaisey stuffed the gun back in his pack. He coughed, wishing Morris would put out his pipe. "Before you go, Mr. Houghton, there is one thing we need to address. Do you know why your wife was here shortly before her death? Her footsteps led directly up the hill from here and I think it unlikely she would be in this valley for any other reason than to come here . . . unless she shared your fondness for the hills, Miss Greaves?"

Houghton sighed. "She hated the hills."

"She'd no business being here," interrupted the manager.

"Anthony, shut up. Adela thought, no matter what I told her about England, about Cumberland, that she would be spending the rest of her life in either one of the smartest parts of London or some eternally lush, green paradise. You could understand it coming from a desert."

"The fells have their own beauty," volunteered Morris.

"Very poetic," said the manager.

"Do you know why she was here at the hut?" Vaisey asked again. "Anyone?"

"She thought Jonathan had come here to see me," said Miss Greaves.

Vaisey waited.

"She thought we were using the hut to, to . . . meet one another."

Richards was staring at Houghton, clenching and unclenching his fist, and for the first time Vaisey noticed a similarity between the two men, and not just their red hair. Cousins maybe? It might explain why Houghton used the little manager's Christian name.

"Were you?"

"No," said Houghton, again staring at Miss Greaves.

The hut was silent but for the murmur and crackle of the fire. The farmer's chair scraped across the stone floor as he finally stood up. "I should go. I should get over the pass to Buttermere before it gets dark. Depending on the weather, you'll have at least a night here."

"We could all go," said Morris.

"I'm not going anywhere," said Richards.

"I'm not about to abandon a crime scene, or a murdered woman's body," said Vaisey.

"Be careful, Jonathan," said Miss Greaves, but Houghton, dipping his head under the low door, ignored her.

"Good luck, old chap," said Morris.

The manager pushed the door shut. "I need to see what food I can find for tonight."

"Mr. Richards? Are you and Mr. Houghton related?"

"Yes, we are, though I don't see how it concerns you, Vaisey. We are half brothers. Same mother, different fathers. I am the older one, yet somehow he ends up with the good looks and a farm and I end up running a shack in the middle of nowhere."

"Thank you." Vaisey picked up his cap. "I need a little air; my lungs are not what they used to be."

Vaisey walked round the hut. The snow had stopped again but what had fallen lent the evening a silvery glow. Footsteps showed where Houghton had tramped away toward the pass, and Vaisey looked for him on the slope that rose over the valley. The farmer, a tiny figure now in the white expanse, seemed to be making good progress, taking great plunging strides to gain height.

He didn't seem awfully fond of his half brother and onetime fiancée. Could he have been the killer? Vaisey had seen a great many attempts at putting on grief, and Houghton's had seemed genuine enough. Anyway, if he didn't return, Vaisey would know who his man was.

Man? Miss Greaves seemed to have grounds for a grievance, heading for a gorgeous Lakeland wedding until her chap brings home a girl from Palestine. And that manager Richards seemed to have a few chips on his shoulder.

Vaisey sighed. It could be none of those in the hut at all. It could be someone who is long gone. And then where would he be when the police arrived? Trying to explain how he found the body. He doubted his name meant a great deal up here, and there have been occasions when his reputation has snagged on a little knot of resentment in certain officers.

Morris seemed to know him well enough. Morris. An outsider like himself. Vaisey found it hard to understand why he would choose to hike in weather like this, but then, the forecast had made a fool of him, too.

"Taking the air, old chap?" It was Morris. His pipe had gone out and was cupped in the palm of his hand.

"My lungs are not what they used to be. Gas."

Morris tapped his pipe against the wall, the ash stippling the snow. "May I make a suggestion?"

Vaisey realized how close Morris was standing to him. He removed his gaze from the hills and his eyes met Morris's.

"I think you should leave this matter to the police," said Morris.

"You think Cumbria's finest will solve this?"

"Probably not. She's foreign, after all. But why do you care? Nobody here is a paying client."

"Why would you ask me this, Morris?"

"You know, you may be putting yourself, and indeed all of us, in danger, if the killer thinks someone is on his tail." Morris took a step back and patted Vaisey on the shoulder. "I'll try to stick to smoking outside from now on."

"Thank you," said Vaisey. He let out a long breath and Morris headed back to the hut's door.

Why not just wait for the police? Nobody had asked him to start poking about, not even the husband. And yet he couldn't simply let that poor girl's death go unsolved.

He would start with a proper look at the body. He glanced up at the pass; the light was fading but he could see Houghton near the top now, still slogging upwards.

* * *

THE LIGHT IN THE shed was poor. A single filthy window looked straight out on a stand of glum conifers that would have kept even the brightest sunshine off the shed. He should have asked Richards for a lamp, but he'd rather let them guess at what he was doing out here than tell them.

Forgive me, Mrs. Houghton, he thought and began a second search of her pockets. Three pennies, a shilling, and a farthing in one. A set of keys in another; a freshly laundered handkerchief poked out of the sleeve of her blouse. In the inside pocket of her coat was a notebook. He opened the book and moved to the window to read it.

There was a list of dates, each with a figure beside it, starting with one from roughly a year ago—11.11.21. That one had the figure 10 beside it. Most of the figures were smaller than this and one or two were followed by a question mark, as if she were guessing. The dates were all between a week and a month apart and took up barely two pages. The rest of the book was empty, but for a name, Fisher, and a London phone number.

He looked again at the folded paper from her wallet. William Eugene Johnson was a onetime American lawman and now director of the London office of the World League Against Alcoholism. Vaisey remembered the day when police had had to rescue him from a mob of students in the capital. And, of course, the drinks industry hated him. Vaisey had seen the brewers' posters in London, railing against the meddling Yankees and extolling the healthy benefits of regular drinking.

Perhaps Mrs. Houghton, coming from a culture where almost no one drank, had taken up the Prohibition cause. But you would not kill her for it, would you?

He tucked the book and poster in his own pocket and replaced the keys and cash in her coat.

Standing by the window, he realized what had struck him as so odd about the shed. From the outside, the window appeared to be halfway along the shed wall, but inside it was only a few inches away. He pulled aside some of the logs and tapped his knuckles on the wall behind them. It was just cheap board, not the heavy creosoted timbers he would have expected. Working quickly now, he pulled more logs aside but could see no break in the board to indicate a way into whatever lay behind it. He replaced the logs and draped the blanket back over Mrs. Houghton.

It was almost dark now but there was light enough to walk down the side of the shed and round to the window. He was right. There was at least eight feet of wall beyond the window. The hidden chamber was easily large enough to hide a pair of horses. He pushed at the planks all along the wall, but nothing moved.

A large crooked nail, smeared with paint, protruded about halfway down. It slipped out easily when he wiggled it. Looking closely at where it had emerged, he saw a hole that went straight through the bottom of the plank and into the top of the one below it. He pulled at the top plank. Now liberated from those below, he found that the plank, along with those above it, swung outward on a hinge. Holding them open, he peered inside.

At least twenty wooden barrels were stacked in the chamber, and, amid the scents of wood and dirt, he could smell whisky. He pushed himself up on tiptoe and saw in the gloom at the bottom of the chamber a pair of latches that he assumed would allow the bottom half of the wall to be lifted aside altogether. This would make loading the hidden store easy.

He pulled his head out, lowered the hinged planks, and replaced the nail. Brushing cobwebs and dust from his sleeve, he turned to follow the trail of footprints into the conifers.

When he reached the wood, he glanced back once more at the shed. A weak light trembled in the window. Someone had gone in there just after him.

Vaisey shrank against the nearest tree as a dark profile appeared at the window. The head appeared to grow as whoever it was pushed their face closer to the glass and stared out. At this distance, in failing light and through the filthy glass, the face was unrecognizable.

Remaining utterly still, he could not tell if he had been seen. He waited until the face dropped away from the window before he slipped between the trees and on to a path of pine needles. The dense conifers had kept out the snow, but they also kept out the light and Vaisey was wishing he had done this earlier. There were woods like this all over Lakeland where the Forestry Commission had marched regiments of pines into every valley and even on to some of the fells. Left to grow for thirty years and of no interest to naturalists or walkers, they were the perfect hiding place.

He reached a spot where a single tree had been felled to create a little space. A canvas awning was slung between the neighboring trunks and beneath it was the ash of a small fire and a muddle of large glass jars and tubes. The whole setup appeared not to have been used for at least a few days. Vaisey was no expert on brewing spirits, but he believed he was looking at a still, a faint whiff of alcohol mingling with the forest's resinous air. Someone was making spirits out here and didn't want anyone to know about it.

Somewhere behind him a piece of wood snapped. He froze, ears whistling in the silence. A pair of pigeons dropped on to a branch above the still and shuffled closer together. Another flapped heavily down into a tree above the path, a black shape against the fading light. He relaxed a little and stooped down to the fire. This must have been where the smoke was coming from that he saw from the mountain. It was cold now, but at the edge of the gray ash he saw a scrap of scorched wool and, attached to it, a strip of fur. The cuff of a glove or coat perhaps?

Who would be brewing out here? It wasn't as if there was a shortage of the real thing. One still like this wouldn't fill all those barrels in the shed. Perhaps there were more hidden away in these forests where little else lives or grows and no one visits, all churning out spirits. Then there would be some real money involved. Hundreds of pounds, even enough to kill for? Maybe that was what Adela Houghton had stumbled upon months ago when she walked here to see what her husband was up to with Miss Greaves.

Vaisey shuddered. The chilly darkness seemed to have crept up on him, as if it had risen through the forest floor. He needed to get back to the hut. Time to ask a few questions perhaps.

He was nearly out of the woods when he heard a faint intake of breath and a rustle of clothing. He ducked, a wartime reflex as sharp as it was years ago. A whisper of troubled air touched his bare scalp as something passed over his head. He backed up a little. There was Richards, both hands on the handle of an axe, trying to tear it from the tree where at least an inch of the blade was clamped in the wet wood of the trunk.

Vaisey had only one weapon, his fists. He jabbed twice, striking Richards's eye with the first blow. Richards cried out and let go of the axe, blocking Vaisey's second blow with the palm of his hand before turning and running.

Vaisey took a deep breath and waited for his racing heart to steady itself. He wished he had his pistol, but it was back in the hut, in his bag, and all of them had seen him offer it to Houghton.

He grabbed the axe handle with both hands and began pushing and pulling it to and fro until the pine tree let it go. A weapon of sorts.

It had probably been Richards in the hut, and he knew about the still. Maybe they were all in it. Morris and the lovely Miss Greaves with her connections to the liquor industry. Return to the hut and they might simply kill him. Wait out here and he'll freeze to death. Try to leave? It was dark now, he didn't know the way, and the snow had started up again. He would go back to the hut, take his chances.

He slipped out of the trees and reached the woodshed. Still holding the axe, he crossed a patch of fresh snow and stood by the accommodation hut wall a few feet from the door. He could hear voices.

"He's been out to one of the stills . . . and I think he got in the store." It was Richards.

"His gun's here," said Miss Greaves. "You should have just waited until he had finished nosing around and then shot him. Who knows where he is now?"

"He won't get far," said Morris. "Give me the pistol. I can track him in this snow."

Vaisey didn't wait to hear the answer but knew now that he was alone out here. And what about Houghton? He seemed genuine enough about his wife, but what if he never came back?

He shrank back against the wall of the hut as he heard the door open. Morris's silhouette was as sharp against the snow as if it had been cut from black stone. In his right hand was Vaisey's revolver. "Vaisey? Where are you?" he said in a loud whisper. "We need to speak."

He was just far enough away to be able to squeeze off a shot before Vaisey could swing the axe. He strode away from the hut and disappeared. He must be heading for the still or the woodshed.

Vaisey pushed himself from the wall, crunched across the snow, and pulled open the door to the hut.

Richards sat with his back to him. Miss Greaves sat opposite nursing a drink in a crude glass. She looked up and started. Richards must have seen something in her face, turning in his seat as Vaisey slid the door's heavy bolts home. Morris was locked out.

They said nothing as Vaisey, still holding the axe, moved to the fireplace, his back and legs tingling as the heat spread through his body. "No idea I'd got so cold," he said. "I know a little more about what's been going on here now, so now one of you can tell me who murdered Adela Houghton."

Miss Greaves had regained her composure. She took a sip from her whisky and placed the tumbler carefully down in front of her. "What are you going to do? Behead us if we don't speak?"

Vaisey hefted the axe high, letting his right hand slide along the handle as he brought the blade down in a wide arc on the drink, showering the pair of them with whisky and shards of glass.

"I might." Vaisey pulled the blade out of the table, passing it in front of Richards's face. "I did far worse in the war." Richards's eyes followed the bright edge of the blade. He'd be the one to speak first.

Miss Greaves brushed glass and whisky from the front of her coat. "Morris will be back, he's just as much a soldier as you. And he's got your gun."

"All right, all right." Richards spoke up. "It was Morris. He went up the hill after her, after she left here . . . after she told us what she had found."

"And what did she tell you? That she had found your still, that she had kept a note of all those barrels in the shed?" Vaisey lowered the axe; he hadn't really known what he was going to do with it next anyway.

Miss Greaves laughed. "You really think someone would kill her for a few barrels of whisky?"

"So, why was she killed?"

There was a bang at the door. "Let me in." It was Morris.

"Say anything and I will use this," whispered Vaisey, raising the axe again and wondering if he sounded convincing enough. "Face away from the door."

"Let me in, Richards," shouted Morris. "I can't find him. He must have made a run for it." Vaisey slipped across the room and stood with his back to the wall. To one side of him was the door, to the other a small square window, its single pane of glass almost as filthy as the one in the woodshed.

"He's in here, he's in here," shouted Miss Greaves.

Morris's face appeared at the window, inches from Vaisey. The detective jabbed the blunt heel of the axe backwards through the glass. Cold air, snow, and shattered glass spilled into the hut as Morris dropped back into the darkness with a cry.

Vaisey had only seconds before Morris recovered. He flung back the bolts on the door. There, in the weak yellow light from the hut, was Morris on his back in the snow. Blood leaked from between his fingers as he held one hand to his face. Vaisey scooped up his revolver and brushed away the snow from the trigger guard.

"You've broken my nose, you bastard."

"Get in the hut. Or stay out here, I don't much care."

* * *

VAISEY HAD EXPECTED MISS Greaves to tend Morris's face, but she had poured herself another drink and sat watching the detective. Richards handed Morris an old pillowcase to stem the bleeding.

"You going to keep the gun on us all night?" said Miss Greaves.

"If I have to."

"We'll just tell the police that you killed Adela. Three witnesses against one. Who are they going to believe? An impostor like you, or her brother-in-law and myself? My family is well-known in Cumbria."

Vaisey sat down. "I could do with some tea."

Richards hesitated.

"Why not?" said Miss Greaves.

Richards went into the kitchen. Vaisey knew he could pick up a knife or some other weapon in there, but he had the revolver and, anyway, he doubted Richards had the guts for anything like that. Morris was hunched over the table, holding the pillowcase to his face. Miss Greaves toyed with her whisky, the fireplace behind her. She certainly liked a drink.

With a jolt, Vaisey realized the old shotgun was missing from the wall. Someone must have moved it while he was outside.

Richards returned. "No tea, I'm afraid, Vaisey. But I found this." He was holding the old gun, aiming it squarely at Vaisey's face, his pink cheek squashed against the dirty brown stock. At such close range, he could not miss, and though Vaisey still doubted Richards would pull the trigger, he wasn't prepared to risk it. He could easily shoot before Vaisey could bring his revolver to bear.

"Shoot him now," said Miss Greaves.

"You know, that's a very old gun," said Vaisey.

"Anthony . . . shoot him."

"Even if it works, the barrels will be pitted inside and rusty. They'll probably blow, take half your face off. But Miss Greaves doesn't seem awfully worried about that."

Richards lowered the gun slightly. "She's never been concerned about anybody . . . except maybe my stupid brother. She just needed me . . ."

"Oh, for God's sake," Miss Greaves said.

"To help with this whisky business?"

"Whisky?" said Morris through the pillowcase. "That's something of an exaggeration. The Americans have a name for it. Moonshine."

"Your people in London are happy enough to buy it," snapped Miss Greaves.

Richards sighted the shotgun on Vaisey again. "Give me your revolver."

Vaisey picked up the revolver by the barrel and lay it on the table in front of Richards. He assumed he was out of danger for at least a few minutes . . . or at least until Morris recovered.

"Allow me to develop a theory," he started. "Mrs. Houghton thinks her husband has renewed his friendship with Miss Greaves and in trying to keep tabs on him, stumbles across what's going on here. She disapproves of alcohol and—"

"Too right she does, meddling bloody foreigner," said Richards. "And then she gets in with that prohibition crowd—"

"Anthony, shut up. Let the man peddle his theory."

"Mrs. Houghton kept a record of all the comings and goings. Did you know that? You must have more than half a dozen stills dotted round this valley, dutifully tended by Richards while he runs this walkers' hostel or hut or whatever it is. You with your trade connections, Miss Greaves, are feeding this moonshine—as Morris likes to describe it—out to your pubs, perhaps to adulterate the real stuff, Scotch from over the border. Now you're doing so well with it, Morris is up from London to do a spot of buying for . . . who knows, pubs, clubs . . . criminals?"

"If only you knew," said Morris.

"I have heard enough. Shoot him, Anthony."

Richards took aim for a third time. "Sorry, Vaisey."

Vaisey sat utterly still. He'd survived five years in the trenches, bombardments that left him with seamless tinnitus, and a gas attack that had scarred his lungs and killed his hair, only to be shot by a little pink man in an apron.

"Do it," urged Miss Greaves.

Richards squeezed the trigger. There was a click. He tried the second trigger. Another click as the hammer dropped on an empty chamber. Vaisey dared to breathe again, his chest aching as he drew a great gasp of air and lunged for his revolver.

Richards snapped open the old shotgun. "Who the devil . . . ?"

Miss Greaves glared at him. "Anthony, you're an imbecile."

Morris held up a pair of brick-red shotgun cartridges. "You must be looking for these." He managed a smile through a mask of caked blood.

"Morris, what are you doing?" said Richards.

Morris stood up. "My name is not Morris. It's Fisher. Inspector Craig Fisher of Her Majesty's Customs and Excise, conducting an investigation into a trade in unlicensed liquor and links with the London underworld. Until Vaisey arrived, I was wondering if I would be the next to get my throat cut. Instead, I got my nose bashed in."

"I had no idea," said Vaisey. "And I'm awfully sorry about your nose."

"I tried to tell you."

"You did?"

"At first I thought your meddling would queer my pitch, even get me killed, but when Houghton left and you found that whisky—something I'd not managed—I thought I'd let you run with it."

There was a clatter as Richards threw down the gun before slumping into his seat. Miss Greaves stared into her drink.

Vaisey ran his hand over his head. "You could have intervened a little earlier, Morris—Fisher, I mean. I thought I was going to get it then."

"I know, but after what you did to my face, I was quite enjoying the show."

Vaisey grunted. "There's two things we need to tie up. Firstly, Houghton. Does he know about this whisky business? And what about his wife's murder?"

Fisher shrugged. "He's part of this business, but my guess is, he wasn't part of his wife's murder."

"We'll have to ask him all about it when he gets here."

Miss Greaves looked up from her drink. "I killed her."

Richards was on his feet. "Emilia, please don't say that. I killed Adela Houghton."

"Make your bloody minds up," said Fisher.

Miss Greaves put a hand on Richards's forearm. "It's all right, Anthony, we're finished here."

"You are, indeed, Miss Greaves. I had a very good idea who killed Adela Houghton. The footsteps leading way from her body on the hill were small, almost certainly those of a woman. There was whisky spilt on the rock shelf where you stood waiting for Adela Houghton—no one in this select group seems to have quite such a taste for it as you—and when we went up the mountain to fetch her down, you knew how she had died."

Fisher picked up the shotgun. "Nobody likes a know-it-all, Vaisey."

"There is also the matter of her gloves. She doesn't appear to have any. Presumably there was an attempt to destroy them in the fire in the woods after they became stained with blood." Vaisey held up the strip of fur-lined fabric he had found outside. "By the way, Fisher, your name was in Mrs. Houghton's notebook."

"She was our contact. She got in touch with the police and they gave it to us and then I got in touch with her husband . . . pretended to be a buyer."

Vaisey watched Miss Greaves finish her drink. He took away her glass. "One wonders how much affection was left between Houghton and a wife who was prepared to betray him to the police."

"Another question for Houghton?"

"I don't think Adela Houghton was killed because she found the liquor and went to the police, or her prohibitionist ideals, or because she was an outsider, a foreigner. They were just excuses; perhaps Miss Greaves here thought they were excuses enough to get her back into the affections of Jonathan Houghton."

"He would have come back to me," Miss Greaves said quietly. "I waited all through that war for him and I would have kept waiting."

"The war took a great deal from a great many of us, Miss Greaves," said Vaisey. "Richards, you should make that tea now."

Funnybone

William Hemlepp

WHEN MARTIN WOKE UP FLAT ON HIS BACK IN A COLD, METAL ROOM, THE FIRST thing he noticed was the smell. The lack of one. Even if it was too faint to make out consciously, everywhere on the planet had a smell. From the bank to the hardware store, the doctor's office to the beach, the mountains to the night clubs. This absence, this tiny piece missing from the puzzle of his senses, was the first thing that told Martin he wasn't on Earth anymore.

He let out a weak cry as he sat up in one, stiff motion like a doll coming to life, panting the stale air of that scentless room. The concentrated mix of canned oxygen Martin had breathed once while scuba diving filled his throat, making his lungs feel cold. Rolling onto his hands and knees, he blinked sleep out of his eyes and stared down at the metal floor. At least, he *assumed* it was metal. There were no bore marks, no imperfections, no screws or bolts. The room looked more like it had been grown than built.

With barely a sound, a thin seam parted between Martin's hands, forcing him to scramble to his feet. He backpedaled to a corner as dark lines began to reach across the gray walls, turning at angles until they touched into elaborate squares and rectangles. Then, after a moment of hesitation, the metal walls between the lines throbbed, then jolted outward out all at once, making Martin jump.

Where the room had once been uniformly smooth, misshapen lumps of gray metal jutted out from the walls. Martin staggered forward, his eyes on a long shape that took up half the far wall. With a raised back, lumpy seat, and rounded armrests, it only took a few moments of squinting for him to recognize it as a couch, but colorless and untextured, like a couch wrapped entirely in smooth tinfoil.

A tiny circle the size of a shot glass slid open in the ceiling before a multicolored globe connected to a black cable sank through it, dangling above the room like a miniature disco ball. It sparked a bright light like a camera flash, blinding him for a moment. When he rubbed his eyes clear of the red blotch in his vision, Martin found himself standing in a comfortable, dimly lit home office decorated with old furniture, with exception to the flat-screen TV mounted on the wall. *His* home office.

Cupping his hands over his mouth, Martin pinched the bridge of his nose, panting warm breath back against his face as he tried not to hyperventilate. He almost preferred the metal room to the empty facsimile of somewhere he considered safe. It was the terror of the uncanny, of looking at something he recognized and knowing it was a lie.

A quiet metallic beep drew his attention to the office door at his back. The old door, made of dark oak and hanging on polished golden hinges, noiselessly slid straight up into the ceiling instead of opening inward like it should have. A bright spotlight beyond the doorway nearly blinded Martin again, but he had time to block most of it with the back of his hand and save his eyesight. As he lowered his hand, he suddenly wished he hadn't.

A misshapen Something sat at the end of the room, all the more foreign next the familiar surroundings. A gray lump of calloused flesh, bell-shaped, with a long stalk rising up on a thin neck before curving down again. It looked like someone had tried to assemble an elephant in the dark. A huge eye with a cross-shaped pupil blinked at Martin from the center of what he had to call its chest, flanked by two arms that ended in boneless tentacles in place of fingers.

Between them, the floor opened up and a metal table rose from beneath the projection of his favorite antique rug. The Something shuffled forward, not on legs but on a bundle of pink cilia that carried it in a smooth, gliding motion across the floor. From somewhere Martin couldn't see, the Something produced a black box the size of a coffee cup, set it on the table, then retreated back to the door, drifting easily backwards without needing to turn away from him. With its back to the wall, it wrapped its tentacles around one another in an oddly human gesture of patience.

With no other option available to him, Martin reached down and picked up the black box without taking his eyes off the Something in the corner. It was lighter than it should have been, barely the weight of a light bulb, and felt brittle enough for a stray sneeze to shatter it. A small groove on one side told him where the lid was, and he worked it open with his fingernail. A tiny object that looked like a baby's pacifier sat on a white cushion, and it neither exploded nor tried to bite him. Martin pinched the object between his fingers and lifted it closer to his eye.

Another light blinked to life to Martin's right and he nearly dropped the tiny device. The TV mounted on the wall had turned itself on. A faceless, hairless mannequin of a human man with overly realistic skin stood onscreen, holding the same object in its hands. Martin watched as the mannequin held the device by the smaller end and inserted the softer, misshapen part into its ear before turning it like a key. It then turned the smaller end counterclockwise before pulling out a thin wire and dragging it to where its mouth should have been.

The motions of the mannequin using the device played over and over again, on loop. Martin glanced at the Something in the corner of the room, squinting at it. With a sigh, he pinched the smaller end of the device, the one shaped like a pill capsule, and copied the motions on the screen. The soft end felt like warm rubber against his skin and quickly expanded to fill his ear cavity when he turned it. The sound was muffled like an earplug on the right side of Martin's head, but after a clear tone beeped inside his head, the sensation disappeared.

Across the room, the Something removed a similar object from a skin pocket below its arms and inserted it into a small hole at the base of its neck. When it dragged the wire to a thin slit just above its eye, Martin did the same toward his mouth. He let go, expecting the wire to fall and dangle off his shoulder like a fishing line, but it remained fixed in place a few inches above his lips. The Something glided forward across the room and uncoiled its tentacles as the metal table sank into the floor.

"Hello."

What Martin heard was a wet, sucking noise like a shower drain trying to talk, but what he understood was the word *hello*.

"Heeehh—Hello," Martin said back.

"Hello," the Something said again. "We are not going to kill you."

"Oh." Martin swallowed. "Good."

"We will return you to your home," it continued. It was getting easier for Martin to ignore the guttural choking noises coming from its mouth and to focus on the words playing into his ear. "You are not a prisoner."

"That's good."

"Would you like something to eat or drink?"

"I'm doing all right, thanks."

"Would you like some time alone?"

"I'm—" Martin hesitated. Now that the Something was speaking to him, he found himself a little more curious than afraid, if in a roundabout way. And only a little. "I don't *think* so?"

The Something made a light gurgling sound and fluttered the tentacles at the ends of its arms.

"*This is an expression of relief and pleasure,*" said a robotic voice in his ear.

"Oh. All right." Martin forced himself to smile, letting out a nervous little chuckle, and hoped the Something was given a similar message.

"I would like to express an apology," the Something said. "You woke up sooner than was anticipated. The intention was for you to find yourself somewhere familiar to alleviate a shock."

"I see." Martin turned in place and looked around his false office. "But . . . wouldn't it be just as shocking if I woke up in my office and an alien walked through the door?"

The Something didn't answer. Instead, it pulled on its tentacles and wound them into knots.

"*This is an expression of embarrassment,*" the device told him.

"Would you like to repeat this encounter?" the Something said. "Would you like your memory of this first encounter suppressed so we may implement your suggestions?"

"N-No, that's all right. I'll . . . I'll manage."

"Understood." The Something glided forward a few feet and gestured to the couch. "Would you like to sit?"

"*This is an expression of invitation.*"

"Is there a way to turn that off?" Martin asked, pointing to the device in his ear.

"No. Would you like to sit?"

"*This is an expression of invitation.*"

Martin was growing more irritated than afraid. The Something was starting to seem less like an advanced alien intelligence and more like a socially awkward party host. It at least had the effect of tapering off his fear.

The couch was soft but felt more like sitting on a plastic bag than an actual cushion. The Something moved across from him and stood patiently as a flat disc rose a few feet out of the floor. When it sat, the disc bulged outward at the sides like a beanbag chair.

"Please feel free to ask your most pressing questions," it said.

"Okay. Um." Martin flopped back against the couch and sighed, running his fingers through his hair. "Jesus, what the fuck?"

"I do not know the answer to that question."

"I didn't— That wasn't a question." Martin pursed his lips and frowned at the alien's eye. An encyclopedia's worth of questions swirled around his mind, enough to make him dizzy. Every time he tried to ask something, another question bubbled up to take its place and gnawed at his curiosity. Finally, after minutes of flapping his lips like a dying fish, Martin asked the first question that came out of his mouth.

"Why aren't you wearing clothes?"

The eye in the center of the alien spun in its socket, then widened.

"This is an expression of confusion."

"Is it a *species* thing? A *culture* thing?" Martin pinched his shirt. "I mean, humans wear clothes all the time, so why . . . Hang on, where are my shoes?" He leaned over his knees and saw his bare toes wiggling on a floor that looked like carpet but still felt like cold steel.

"Your shoes carried too many harmful bacteria and were atomized. I apologize if they were of sentimental value to you. As for clothing, my people generally only wear them during special occasions or for religious ceremonies." After a beat, the Something added, "Would you like time alone to grieve for your shoes?"

Martin shook his head, already kicking himself for wasting a question on something stupid.

"Am I . . . Are we in space?" he asked.

"We are orbiting concurrently with your planet's moon and docked behind it."

"So, on the far side of the moon." Martin suddenly felt dizzy and gripped the edge of the couch. "Christ almighty."

"Thank you for not screaming," the alien said, wiggling its tentacles again. "Seventy-eight percent of humans scream when being presented with this information."

"I think I'm going to throw up." A small basin rose out of the floor next to Martin's leg.

"Eighty-nine percent of humans react similarly."

He felt dizzy, imagining all that space between himself and home, like he were an insect being dangled above the Grand Canyon.

However, curiosity once again took over his instincts and he felt the copper taste in the back of his throat begin to subside.

"I'm . . . okay. I think I'm okay." He took a deep breath of the plastic air, held it for a moment, then exhaled. "It's just . . . it's a lot to take in."

"I understand."

Martin squinted at the alien's eye, a fat plus-sign surrounded by a jagged iris of deep blues and greens. Maybe he was allowed a little shock, given the circumstances, but his host had been nothing but polite and deserved a little courtesy.

"What's your name?"

The alien opened its mouth and let out a low piping sound that Martin could feel in his chest, something halfway between the braying of a donkey and a broken foghorn.

"*Untranslatable*," the device said.

Martin winced and dug a finger into his free ear.

"I apologize, I misunderstood your question. Please refer to me as J."

"J? Like the letter J?"

"It is the closest approximation to my given name."

"Sure. J. Got it." Martin sighed, at that point willing to just accept whatever the alien told him. He held out his hand, though he realized J might not understand the gesture. To Martin's surprise, J extended a gray, rubbery arm and took his hand, wrapping the soft tentacles around his fingers before giving him a friendly shake. Martin smiled, trying not to shudder at the damp residue J had left in his palm.

"Well, if I have your name, you might as well have mine."

"You are Dr. Martin Lancaster, professor of cultural anthropology at the University of Notre Dame."

Martin was startled, but decided it wasn't surprising an alien capable of plucking him out of his bedroom in the middle of the night would know what was on his business cards.

"Please confirm this information."

"Yeah, yes. Yes, that's me." Martin moved to take off his coat, getting as comfortable as he possibly could while two hundred thousand miles above the planet. "I guess if you bothered to get my name, then this isn't going to turn into a probing, at least."

J's eye spun in its socket again. Martin didn't need a translator to tell him that a joke hadn't landed.

"Uh . . . anyway. If I'm not about to be *dissected* or anything like that," Martin folded his arms and shrugged, "what am I doing here?"

J let out a high-pitched trill that the translator informed him meant excitement. It glided across the floor as a panel of lights began to glow below the television on the far wall. Martin watched, his arms still folded, as the alien began speaking to itself in short honks and piping sounds the translator repeatedly told him were untranslatable. He began to wonder why he'd ever thought the little creature was intimidating to begin with.

"Dr. Martin Lancaster," J began. Even filtered through the translation device, the words had a weighty air to them. Martin resisted rolling his eyes but allowed himself a weary sigh. He'd been to enough conferences to know when a presentation was coming. "I represent an interplanetary collective founded on research and cultural exchange. We are comprised of seven hundred million members spanning the galaxy, each dedicated to the further enrichment of our shared experience through cultural understanding."

"Uh-huh," Martin said in a flat tone. He half expected this abduction to end with J trying to sell him a time-share.

"My colleagues and I have dedicated our lives to the study of Earth culture and society, our research dating back hundreds of your years. Our methodology prevents us from making official contact before a species has crossed a threshold of development, but exceptions have been made."

"Clearly."

"We have nearly completed our final assessment of the human race, but—" J seemed to break from its rehearsed speech and began tugging at its tentacles once again. "There is a limit to what we can discern through observation."

The television screen lit up above J. On it was an almost impossibly clear image of a middle-aged man sitting on a park bench with a cell phone to his ear. It looked real enough for Martin to climb inside. The image sat frozen for a moment before playing a video of the man clutching the back of the bench to hold himself upright as he laughed, deep and full, his eyes squinted into creases with tears in the corners. It looped twice before changing to another video, one showing three young women in a bathroom together, all giggling hard enough for their faces to turn an identical shade of cherry red. Following it was an old woman on a bus, reading a book in the sun and covering her mouth with her fist as she snickered quietly to herself. Then a group of skinny men in white robes laughing as another man in the distance tried and failed to mount a horse.

The video froze, without a stutter, on the image of the men nearly doubled over with hysterics. J lifted an arm and coiled its tentacles around one another to point at the men.

"What is this?"

"What? Laughter?" Martin cocked his head. "They're laughing."

"We know what the phenomenon is called," J said, "but we have been unable to discern the underlying meaning."

"It's a response to humor," Martin said and slid to the edge of the couch with a frown. Hundreds of years of study and they still hadn't figured out what people did when they saw something funny?

"*Huuuu-mooor*," J said, but not through the translator. The alien pursed its lip-less mouth and tried to mimic the word, but with biology that wasn't built for it.

Martin first thought he was being made fun of, but forced himself to think from his degree instead of his ego. It dawned on him that, like *schadenfreude*, *seppuku*, and *ennui*, J was attempting to use a foreign word to define something their own language wasn't supplied for.

"A response to comedy," he said, testing out different language J might more easily understand. "Like tragedy and comedy."

"We understand tragedy," J said. "But this other concept we have been unable to identify."

"It's— It's *comedy*. We laugh when something's *funny*."

"*Hooh-meh-hee*," J tried to say, but it came out like someone trying to talk through a snorkel. "*Huhn-hee*. We've encountered these words before, but had no correlating meaning to which to assign them." J coiled its collection of tentacles around each other like a bundle of rope, which the translator in Martin's ear told him meant embarrassment.

"No correlating meaning?" Martin's brow furrowed and he tapped a finger to his bottom lip. "Do you . . . not know what *humor* is?"

J glanced back up at the screen with its huge eye. "It has been the greatest obstacle in our understanding of human life."

"Not war or racism or violence or anything like that," Martin said. "It's *humor* that you can't figure out?"

"I have written essays on human war," J said, brightening with excitement as the topic seemed to shift to something it knew about. "The topic is simple once understood in context."

Martin stood from the couch and paced the room, the cold of the false carpet chilling his bare feet.

"You understand *emotion*, don't you?" he asked. "Joy, sadness, anger, fear."

"Yes. With few exceptions, every developed race of sufficient sentience in the known galaxy has adapted some form of emotional response."

"But not humor?" Martin stopped his pacing and folded his arms. "Seven hundred million researchers, and humans are the *only* race you've found that knows how to laugh?"

"It is, frankly speaking, your most unique trait."

He chewed on the tip of his thumb before turning to J and looking eyes-to-eye with the alien.

"All right, let's say that someone you know, your friend, is doing something. Making something. They drop it and it breaks. How do you feel?"

"I feel terrible for them and I would attempt to help if I am able," J said, the translator in Martin's ear failing to communicate more than the flat, emotionless tone of an airline attendant.

"Right. Okay. Now let's say this friend is cooking, maybe some kind of sauce." Martin wondered if J's species even ate the way his did, but decided to just stick with the story. "They cook it wrong and the sauce *explodes* all over your friend's face. What do you do?"

"I express sympathy at the ruined meal and assist with cleaning up." J's eye spun in puzzlement. "Is one of these scenarios meant to spark this emotion?"

"Uh. Well. I mean." Martin coughed into his hand. "Bad example."

"We are aware that this emotional response is linked to joy and happiness of some kind," J said, "but the variables are too unpredictable to establish a pattern."

"People laugh for all kinds of reasons," Martin said. "Most people do it at something funny, but some people laugh when they're nervous or afraid, as a stress relief. Some people laugh more in groups while some laugh more when they're alone. And what different people find funny is so varied there's really no way to pin it down. You can't be an *expert* at what's funny. There's no equation you can put data into and come out with a joke."

"But you have specialists," J said. "You are one yourself, Dr. Martin Lancaster."

"A specialist? A specialist in what?"

For an answer, J turned to the television screen. The picture was crystal clear, recorded with technology far surpassing what humans were capable of, which made it doubly impressive considering the footage was from almost twenty years ago. The frozen image of the laughing men was replaced with one of Martin, standing onstage in a dimly lit bar in front of a dingy red curtain.

"S-so I go up to the guy, trying to look like a hardass, y'know?" the younger Martin stammered into the microphone with a grin on his face held there only by nerves. He shuffled in place, a worn pair of Converse All-Stars squeaking on the stage, and gripped the mic stand so hard his knuckles were turning red. "And I say, 'Look, if you wanna fuck my mom that bad, you can just go ahead!'"

The delivery was strained and painful, but there wasn't much worse that could be done to an already bad joke. You could see the fear in Martin's eyes in the scant few seconds before the audience gave him a pity laugh and a polite round of applause. He was already moving into another joke, without even giving the first time to land, but the present-day Martin had willed himself into deafness through nothing but the power of shame.

"*Oh my God,*" he said, sinking his fingers into his scalp as every drop of blood in his body rushed to his face. This was, by magnitudes, the most horrifying thing he'd seen all day. "*Turn it off.*"

J stopped the video on a frame of the younger Martin in mid-laughter at his own joke, a memory he recalled more vividly than his own wedding day.

"Where . . . *Where* did you get that?" Martin spat while pointing at the screen.

"Through a reconnaissance drone," J said. "Though the video has been stored in our records for some time."

"Delete it." Martin's eyes widened with madness. "*Please.* I am *begging you* to delete this video."

J hesitated, balling its tentacles into knots and turning between Martin and the screen.

"Our organization has restrictions against the unauthorized purging of research data."

"I don't want any*one* or any*thing* in the known universe to see that stand-up routine again."

"I was unaware the presentation of this data would cause you distress, but I cannot—"

"So help me God, I will crash this ship into the moon if I have to." Martin stole a glance at his early-twenties self and found himself wishing he *had* been dissected.

J's eye spun in its socket while the alien paced a small circle on the floor. Finally, it made a sound like a dying trumpet and raised an arm to the control panel on the wall.

"*This is an expression of resignation,*" the translator told Martin as J pressed a red button and the video on screen dissolved into millions of digital particles. Only once it was gone did the invisible hand around Martin's lungs relax its grip. Now, the only records of that set existed in the memories of Martin, his unfortunate audience, and Satan (because God certainly wouldn't have let it happen if He had been there).

"I apologize for causing you distress," said J, whose proxy voice seemed to carry a new edge of irritation. "But please explain your emotional response."

"There is nothing in the world more horrible than comedy done badly," Martin said, gravely serious. "Is *that* why I'm here? Because I tried to do stand-up in college?"

"Partially. Your field of academic study is the closest approximation to our mission, and your experience as a specialist in . . . " J hesitated before piping out another attempt at the word *humor*, "make you uniquely qualified for our purposes."

"I made fifteen dollars from that set," Martin said, mostly to himself. "And then it got me abducted by aliens. Fantastic."

When he realized J was staring at him, Martin picked at his fingers and shrugged. "Look, I'm probably the farthest thing from an expert as you can get. Comedy is hard. Some people are good at it, but there's more to it than it seems. There's timing, there's body language, there's delivery. A good joke can be ruined by telling it wrong. You can't point to something and say 'That is objectively funny.' You know it when you see it."

Martin dropped his hands to his sides and frowned at the alien, seeing his words were going in through one sound orifice and out the other. It would've been easier to explain music to the deaf. Would J and the other aliens let him leave if he couldn't get them to understand? Did Martin's freedom depend on his ability to make a group of space aliens laugh when he could hardly get his fellow humans to do the same? He hadn't gotten stage fright in years, but Martin could feel the tight ache in his chest like it had never left.

His eyes drifted from J to the blank television on the wall. Chewing on the tip of his thumb, he strode toward it while an idea took shape with every step.

You know it when you see it. Of course *explaining* the concept of humor wasn't going to work. Nobody laughed at a joke when you told them *why* it was funny. It just had to happen on its own.

"Those videos, the ones of people laughing," Martin said. "How many more of them do you have?"

"Roughly fifteen million hours of footage," J said. "Cataloged by Earth year."

"Can you bring them back up?"

J complied, tapping on the wall control until the screen lit up on a picture of men in petticoats and powdered wigs laughing around a dinner table lit with candles.

"Oh. Can we . . . How about more recent footage? From the last twenty years."

"That narrows the selection considerably."

"Comedy doesn't age well."

J responded with a puzzled stare before complying, the picture onscreen changing to show two old men sitting on a bench and surrounded by an urban sprawl with nearby street signs written in Chinese. Martin nodded to himself and crossed to the couch to get as comfortable as he could next to his discarded coat.

"Come sit," he said, inviting J over with a wave. "Let's see what you have."

"We have reviewed much of this data already," J said.

"But not with me."

The alien tugged on its tentacles for a moment before slowly crossing the room and settling next to the couch. The furniture wasn't built for J's body, but it seemed comfortable enough on the floor. It was the closest Martin had been to the creature, and he had to fight the urge to stare.

The videos were all only a few seconds apiece, just long enough to capture the beginning and end of a fit of laughter. Most of them only showed the end of a joke or the immediate aftermath of whatever sent the human subjects into hysterics. Even more were just clips of people laughing at television or movie screens without any attention paid to what was actually on them. The aliens clearly didn't know what they were looking for.

After nearly two dozen short snippets of video, there was one that finally made him chuckle. A group of young children were playing soccer in a dusty park, somewhere in South America, and taking turns kicking the ball toward a chalk square drawn on a brick wall. One of them, a few years older than the others, carried the ball forward with impressive footwork before driving it into the center. It hit the wall, bounced back with equal force, and hit the boy square in the forehead, knocking him off his feet with his body stiff as a board.

Martin snorted, jumping at the unexpected conclusion and laughing deep in his throat along with the other boys as their older friend rolled onto his feet with a sore head and bruised ego. Beside him, Martin found J staring at him with its enormous eye. He stopped laughing and cleared his throat before turning back to the screen.

Martin couldn't begin to guess where the aliens had hidden their "drones," but there were evidently thousands of them judging on the variety in the recordings. Most of the clips were useless, but within the hours and hours of archived video were brilliant gems of slapstick comedy. A man in a tuxedo falling down a flight of stairs. A woman sneezing into a milkshake and splattering whipped cream across her face. The sight of a bus driving down a busy street with a man's arm half stuck in the closing doors. It was base humor, the kind of physical comedy that could entertain a toddler, but Martin laughed all the same.

J sat quiet and still beside him, only moving to glance between Martin and the screen. It should've felt odd enough that he was watching cheap renditions of *America's Funniest Home Videos* with a one-eyed alien, but what troubled Martin most of all was the silence. He'd grown all to accustomed to the sight of people *not* laughing while up onstage and couldn't ignore the nervous fluttering in his heart.

Martin's favorite clip so far was taken from a snowy city street with steely gray concrete and wet slush in every direction, likely somewhere in Russia. A middle-aged man with a stony, serious expression trudged down the sidewalk with two young boys following in the footsteps he left in the snow. He fished a set of keys from his jacket pocket and began to climb the stone steps to an apartment building. When one of his feet slipped out from under him, he dropped the keys into the snow and caught himself on the handrail.

The way the man slipped brought a smile to Martin's face, but what made him laugh even harder was how the man *kept* slipping. Over and over again, he tried to regain his balance on the bottom step only for his feet to slip out from under him each and every time. He wobbled and pitched, gripping the metal handrail while running in place like he was stuck on a treadmill. Martin's chuckles descended into a full belly laugh at absurdity at just *how long* this man had spent falling. He was cackling along with the two little boys in the video like he wasn't a year older than they were.

"*HOORK HOORK HOORK HOORK HOORK.*"

Martin nearly fell off the couch as J let out a harsh gasping sound like a walrus being strangled. It trembled and wheezed on the floor, its huge eye hidden behind a thick, leathery lid. The alien seemed to be gasping for breath, hugging itself with its long arms.

"*This is an expression of . . . This is an expression of . . . This is an expression of . . .*"

The translator couldn't make sense of what was happening, but Martin recognized it immediately. He grinned.

J stopped convulsing after nearly a minute and blinked up at Martin, its eye moist with tears that stained the gray skin underneath it.

"I don't understand," said J, tugging anxiously at its pink feelers. "I don't understand. I don't understand."

"I think you just had a giggle fit," Martin said. "You were laughing."

"I don't understand. This has never happened to me before. I don't understand." J was wheezing, its thin lips flapping while it mumbled to itself.

"How did it feel?" Martin asked.

J stopped tugging on its tentacles and swiveled back to the screen. It lurched and made one more gasping *hoork* sound before looking at Martin again.

"I don't know," J said before *hoorking* again. "It feels. Pleasurable. While you were . . . expressing yourself, I began to feel joy at watching that human struggle. And then. And then. Then I."

"Do you . . . want to keep watching?" Martin gestured to the screen. J blinked at him, its mouth half open in a surprisingly human moment of vulnerability.

"Yes."

A switch had been flipped inside the alien's mind. With every new clip of a laughing human, J joined in with a honking cackle of its own. After a while, Martin found himself watching the creature more than the screen, and it was so much easier to laugh alongside J than by himself. He noticed that, like a toddler, J was trembling at the beginning of each clip, already giggling at the mere anticipation of laughter.

"It hurts," J said after a particularly hard peal of their newly discovered laughter. "It is painful to my lungs, but I am enjoying it. I don't understand."

"It happens. Just breathe."

"I have watched this archival research many times, but I have never felt this way. Why am I experiencing joy at the suffering of these humans?"

"Well, there's a bit of a threshold," Martin said. He drew an imaginary line in the air with his finger. "It's funny to watch someone fall down or make a fool of themselves, but it *stops* being funny once someone gets hurt."

"I don't want to enjoy others' pain," J said.

"Nobody said you had to. Most of those people aren't, they're laughing at what someone said. A joke or something."

"What is that?" J asked, almost bouncing with excitement. "What is a '*jho-hook*'?"

"It's basically a story you tell to make someone laugh." He paused and rubbed the back of his neck. "Or *try* to make someone laugh."

"I would like to hear a *jho-hook*," J said, already trembling. "Please tell me a *jho-hook*."

"Oh. Uhh. I mean, I can . . ." Martin cleared his throat. "Most of them are . . . you have to know some context to really . . ."

"I have attained the human equivalent of seven doctorate degrees in the study of Earth culture. Please tell me a jho-hook."

Martin felt his mouth turn dry. This was uncomfortably close to performing again. At least J didn't have a plastic cup to fling at him once he started to bomb.

"Uh, okay. Sure. Let me think." He racked his brain for a joke, preferably someone else's material. "Okay. Okay, here's a good one. There are two hunters out in the woods. One of them—"

"*HOORK HOORK HOORK HOORK.*"

"No. Stop. It's not at the funny part yet."

"I apologize."

Martin cleared his throat.

"Two hunters are out in the woods. One of them suddenly has a seizure and falls over. The first hunter calls the hospital and says, 'My friend is dead, what do I do?' The doctor tells him, 'Don't panic, I can help. First, make sure that he's actually dead.' The doctor then hears a gunshot over the phone and the man says, 'Okay, he's dead. Now what?'"

J erupted into a fit of alien laughter, loud enough that Martin was forced to cover his ears. When J looked like it was about to fall over, he reached out and steadied the alien, its skin rough and cool to the touch. If Martin had gotten this kind of reaction more often, he might not have quit doing stand-up.

"I must report to my colleagues," J said in between gasps and errant honks the translator refused to decipher. "I will not be gone long. Please be patient."

The alien steadied itself and scuttled out the door that opened and closed with a slight *hiss*. Even through the strange metal, Martin could still hear J hoorking down a long hallway before eventually fading from earshot. He settled into the fake couch in his fake office with a self-satisfied grin and used the time to recall any more jokes he remembered.

The door slid open. Martin looked up and expected J, but jumped to his feet as seven other aliens of the same species all glided inside, one after another with J taking up the rear. J was easily the most drab of its colleagues with the other aliens covered in earthy-colored patterns, spots, and stripes. Their eyes were even more vibrant, with irises in a kaleidoscope of color surrounding their cross-shaped pupils.

"Oh. Uhh . . . H-Hey there," Martin said, waving at the group of creatures. They looked closer to bundles of coral than to breathing, thinking beings. None of the seven responded as they sat in a line across from him, blinking dimly and shuffling in place.

J appeared, hurrying down the line with a stack of black boxes in its arms, and passing them out one by one.

"I apologize. I apologize. I apologize," they said to each alien in turn, who each put in its translator in the same manner. Martin noted that whatever organ the aliens listened with was somewhere at the base of their long, trunk-like necks.

"Hello," Martin said again once the aliens could understand him, but this meant he *knew* they were ignoring him when they didn't respond.

"Thank you for coming," J said, repeating it seven times, to each individual in line. J was jittery with excitement and making soft honking noises, the alien's version of an elated giggle. The rest of them, though, were deathly silent, even with the translators in. They made J look practically charismatic, though that may have been why the gray creature was the one sent to meet him in person.

"Dr. Martin Lancaster, please repeat the—*h-hoork*—please repeat the *jho-hook* for my colleagues."

"I . . . Uh . . . okay." Martin cleared his throat and tried not to stutter as he told the joke about the two hunters again. It was already hard enough to read a room without his audience being populated by bug-eyed tentacle monsters.

When he finished, J, and only J, collapsed into a new fit of laughter, just as hard as the first. The other aliens stared at it in what the translator told Martin seven times over were expressions of fear and shock.

"It is—*hoork hoork hoork*—it is because the second human—*hoork*—misunderstood the directives of the medical professional!" J tried to explain to the others through an aftershock of giggles. One by one, the other aliens turned from J to Martin, their gazes taking on a judgmental edge.

"It—It's a little . . . it's dark humor," he stammered. The collar of his shirt had begun to feel very tight, even as he pulled on it. "It's not everyone's thing."

"Are there more? Do you know any more?" J started to laugh again, unprompted, as the other aliens slowly began to back away from them.

"I . . . I don't know *that* many but I . . ." Martin felt the air leaking from his open mouth. He hadn't had this *exact* nightmare before, but it was startlingly close. He took a breath and looked to J, imagining they were the only two people in the room. If even one audience member was laughing, that was something he could work with.

"Here's one. A man is caught fishing illegally by a police officer. The man says, 'I wasn't fishing, officer. These are my pet fish. I take them out here to swim and when they're done, they jump back in the bucket and I take them home.' The officer says, 'I don't believe you, show me.' So, the man one by one puts the fish back in the water, but after a few minutes nothing happens. The officer says, 'Where are all your fish?' and the man responds, 'What fish?'"

Just as before, J's enthusiastic honking filled the room, bouncing off the metal walls, while meeting silence from the rest. They each cast nervous glances at J, who must've seemed like a complete psychotic to them. The one that seemed to lead the others, with an eye the color of volcanic pool and skin spotted like a leopard, squinted at Martin in their species' version of a tight-lipped frown.

"I do not understand," it said. Its translated voice was deeper than J's, but just as flat and mechanical. "What quality makes this scenario pleasurable?"

"I . . . well . . ." Martin stalled, pretending to rub his nose. He wished he were giving a lecture on something he actually understood. "It's . . . It's funny that the man was able to trick the officer in a clever way. And the way he did it is unexpected so, uh . . ."

The alien stared at Martin, unblinking, for a long time.

"I understand," was all it said before turning to one of its colleagues and muttering something out of the translator's range.

"I am—*hoork*—in great pain," J said to Martin, its eye soaked in tears. "But I am enjoying it very much. It is very strange. Please tell us more."

"I'm not exactly an expert at this." The judgmental gaze of the other aliens was starting to make him sweat like he were under a heat lamp. What breakthrough did he make with J? Did they need to *see* comedy to understand it?

While wringing his hands together and racking his brain for another joke, Martin remembered one of the most important keys to good comedy: know your audience. The creatures were about as foreign as an audience could get, but he at least knew they were researchers. Scientists.

"S-so . . . Okay. Here's a—" Martin stopped to swallow past the knot in his throat. Twenty years later and he was bombing just as hard on the dark side of the moon as he did in a South Bend bar on open-mic night. He fixed his gaze on J, who he was convinced would laugh at just about anything at this point, and forced out the stupid, half-remembered pun.

"A nuh-neutron walks into a bar. He asks the buh-b-bartender, 'Hhhh-How much for a beer?' The bartender says, 'For you, no charge.'"

Not even J gave him more than a single, winded *hoork* in response. The other aliens gave less than that. In the thick silence, Martin held his breath, preparing for the moment he'd be fired out into space for crimes against humor.

"*Hoork . . . hoorkhoorkhoork . . .*"

Martin looked to J to thank it for the pity laugh, but the chuckle wasn't coming from J. Instead, it was the blue-striped alien at the farthest end of the room that was starting to laugh. It started as weak honking, but each came harder and louder until it was howling with inhuman cackles like the sound of a broken foghorn.

J burst into a new round of giggles, joining in with the other alien. A third caught the bug and began to snicker alongside them, followed shortly by a fourth, who laughed with deep, bellowing *whoops* Martin could feel in his chest. One after another, the avalanche of laughter cascaded through the room, leaving all eight aliens in hysterics. Last was the skeptical, leopard-spotted creature that nearly doubled-over with a laugh like the hissing of many snakes. The only thing louder than the cacophony around him was the short-circuiting translator in Martin's ear.

"*This is This is This an an an express This ion is an of expression of expression of of of ERROR ERROR ERROR.*" He tried to twist the little device out of his ear, but felt it tug on something very deep inside his skull. Despite this, Martin didn't realize he was laughing as well until he felt his cheeks straining under a broad smile.

"Call the—*hssk hssk hssk hssk*—call the medical—*hssk*—call the medical team," the spotted alien said between gasps.

"Don't," J said, wiggling its tentacles excitedly. "It is not a medical emergency. It is . . ." J struggled to explain the word with a mouth not made for it until Martin finished their sentence.

"It's laughter. You're all laughing."

"I feel weak," said the blue-striped alien as it leaned against a wall to keep itself upright. "I feel dizzy. I feel. Happy."

"I am experiencing great distress," said a copper-red alien, whose untranslated words came out as a disarmingly loud wail. "What is happening?"

"We are exhibiting the symptoms of an adapted strain of the human emotion they refer to as *hu-moor*," J explained to the others, who had finally stopped laughing but seemed winded and exhausted at the effort. "It appears to be communicable between species, as I had hypothesized."

"You have exposed us to infection," said the spotted alien. It stood from the floor and glided toward J as a line of thin, glowing tentacles extended from its back, strobing rapidly.

"*This is an expression of anger,*" the translator told Martin.

"Infection? What infection?" Martin asked.

"My theory was that your concept of '*hu-moor*' functioned similarly to a virus and could only be understood once contracted through direct exposure." J looked up at Martin with an elated gleam in its eye. "It appears that my hypothesis has been proven."

"An *emotional* virus?" Martin reeled, nearly tripping over his own feet. It wasn't just an expression; laughter was, literally, contagious.

"One that the entire outpost has been exposed to," said the spotted alien.

"And it came from us?" Martin tapped the center of his chest. Too many genocides throughout history were linked to a culture's encounter with a simple disease they had no immunity for. Were Martin's stupid jokes the catalyst for an alien pandemic? Was he Patient Zero?

"Evidence suggests your planet was once occupied by a non-human intelligence long before our observation period," J said. "I believe that was your species' first exposure."

"So . . . comedy came from aliens?" Martin's head spun as he flopped onto the couch. "Comedy came from aliens. Of course it did."

"Consider the effects of exposure," J said to the others. "What did your response to Dr. Martin Lancaster's story feel like?"

The spotted alien, still glaring at J, refused to answer, but the blue-striped one spoke in its place.

"It felt. Highly pleasurable," it said. "It was a euphoric episode and I experienced great joy."

"I did not understand what was happening," said a yellow alien with a neon-green eye, "but I did not want it to stop."

"The concept of *hu-moor* is an invasive thought virus, but not a destructive one." J pointed back to Martin, who was slumped across the cushions while still trying to process what he had learned. "Within human society, it has reached full pandemic, but it has also become a cornerstone of their cultural identity. There is reason to believe it has been instrumental to their survival as a species, especially when their exceptionally destructive nature is taken into account."

"I would like to engage in further research on this topic," said the red alien before it turned to look at Martin. The rest followed suit, eight multicolored eyes the size of dinner plates turning his way with an expectant gaze. "Please provide further data."

"Tell us more *jho-hook*," J said, who was gradually growing more accustomed to the word. Seven of the aliens hurried to the couch and crowded around Martin, as excited as toddlers around a birthday clown. Only one alien, the spotted commander, watched with a leering gaze from across the room. The glowing ribbon of light slowly retracted into its back.

"I don't think I have any more," Martin said. "I'm an anthropologist, jokes aren't really my—"

But even as he made the excuse, he knew it wasn't true. He had plenty of jokes, a whole show's worth of them, taking up space in the back of his mind and gathering dust for twenty years. They were awful, less funny now than when Martin first wrote them, but maybe that didn't matter so much twenty thousand miles away from home. The aliens seemed ready to laugh at anything he had to say; they'd gained the ability not even ten minutes ago and were already addicted to comedy.

Martin stood from the couch as his small audience backed away and enclosed him in a semicircle. He brushed off his shirt, cleared his throat, and did whatever else he could think of to stall while trying to remember how his set began. Though, in truth, he'd never forgotten.

"S-So, I was walking back from the bar last night and some asshole jumps out at me with a knife . . ."

Much of Martin's set would've been incomprehensible to his audience. Jokes about South Bend, the college, public figures, and pop culture he left out, along with a few stinkers that never got much of a laugh. However, even with half his show thrown away, J and its colleagues ate up every word. They exploded at every punch line, collapsing into hysterics at every joke like it was the funniest thing they'd ever heard, and it probably was.

Martin had never performed to such an easy crowd; not even his friends were this enthusiastic. He had to stop frequently for them to catch their breath, but it seemed like the aliens were having the time of their lives. They laughed at *everything*. Even as he tried not to cringe at his own terrible material, he puffed out his chest like a proud rooster as his confidence soared. Martin had finally found his audience and they were on the far side of the moon.

". . . I stare at the guy for a minute and tell him, 'I don't care where you're going, get the fuck outta my car!'" Martin shouted, holding one arm out while miming a microphone in the other. It was the last joke of his set and the aliens were rolling over one another, their honking laughter deafening. It was only then that Martin noticed their commander, who had been peering over the others from behind with indignant silence. Every audience had at least one critic, but it still poked a hole in Martin's ego.

"A-All right, that's my set. That's all I have," Martin said with a shrug.

"I am—*hoork*!" J made three attempts to speak while blinking tears out of its huge eye. "I am experiencing overwhelming magnitudes of joy."

"I cannot breathe," said one of the others. "I cannot breathe and I am enjoying it immensely."

"I believe," J said over the laughter of the others, holding out its arms for attention, "I have composed a *jho-hook*." They looked at Martin, as if for permission.

"You have the floor," he said, nodding.

"What is it that *Huezhbez* said to *Ghueniza* when *eer-huahua* was in full *iv'lihua*?"

Martin blinked and fiddled with the translator, but didn't have time to even process J's setup before it immediately delivered the punch line.

"Let us never *uhavala* again!"

Martin could practically hear the wet *slap* as J's joke fell dead on arrival. The other aliens stared in a blank moment of silence before responding with a polite round of pity laughter. Martin joined them.

"Okay . . . that was pretty goo—"

"*HSSK HSSK HSSK HSSK HSSK!*"

Martin jumped along with the rest of the aliens as the commander burst into a wheezing, debilitating fit of laughter. It fell on its side, wiggling its short tentacles in the air as tears pooled on the floor. It almost looked like the commander was in the fit of a seizure as it rolled across the floor until bumping against the far wall. Over time, once its laughter had slowed to a stop, it looked up and found everyone staring at it. Its eye sunk a few inches back into its socket.

"*This is an expression of great embarrassment,*" the translator said.

"Thank you for your cooperation," it said to Martin before sitting up and punching a large, red button on the wall.

The room vanished. For only a moment, Martin could feel himself somewhere between falling and flying at impossible speeds with the kind of velocity that would strip the skin from his bones.

An instant later, he was lying flat on his back in the middle of his front lawn and staring at the cloudless night sky. The grass was wet and tickled the bottoms of his bare feet. His skin was tingling like he'd just spent an hour inside a walk-in freezer. The air was wet, heavy, and smelled of home.

An electric *pop* followed by a bright flash of light made Martin sit up. Out of the light, his abandoned jacket fluttered to the grass beside him, steaming and faintly singed.

When Martin gazed up at the moon, knowing what was on the other side of it, his thoughts weren't of the contact he had made or the things he had seen and learned up there.

He wondered whether the student union still had an open mic night.

Contributors

ALEXANDER WEINSTEIN is the author of the short story collections *Universal Love* (2020) and *Children of the New World*, which was chosen as a notable book of the year by the *New York Times*, NPR, Google, and Electric Literature. Alexander Weinstein's fiction and interviews have appeared in *Rolling Stone, World Literature Today, Best American Science Fiction & Fantasy*, and *Best American Experimental Writing*. He is the director of the Martha's Vineyard Institute of Creative Writing and an associate professor of creative writing at Siena Heights University.

P. JO ANNE BURGH returned to creative writing in her forties, after a twenty-five-year hiatus during which she taught English and creative writing, directed a drama club, studied voice, became a paralegal, went to law school, practiced as a litigator, and established her own practice providing research and writing services to other lawyers. She has also set up a library at a Lahu training center in northern Thailand, argued before the Connecticut Appellate and Supreme Courts, and rescued enough cats over the years to qualify as a cat lady. Jo Anne's short stories have been published in a variety of publications, including TulipTree's *Stories That Need to Be Told 2018*. Both her first novel and her first novella placed as finalists in the 2018 Faulkner-Wisdom Creative Writing Competition. She is currently at work on her second novel.

SANDY LENDER is a magazine editor by day and an author of girl-power fantasy novels by night. Her most recent accomplishment is winning a

2019 Imadjinn Award for Best Literary Fiction Novel. You can check out her author page on Amazon or follow her Facebook page at Fantasy Author Sandy Lender. She lives in Florida, where she volunteers in sea turtle conservation and parrot rescue.

DAVID HOPES's first two novels, *The Falls of the Wyona* and *Night, Sleep, and the Dreams of Lovers*, were released in 2019. He is a writer and painter living in Asheville, North Carolina.

EVAN HUNDHAUSEN is a cannabis journalist and has written for the *Hemp Connoisseur, Dope Magazine*, and Herb.co. He received his MFA in creative writing at Naropa University in 2001. Go find his self-published short story collection on Amazon or visit EvanHundhausen.com.

SHANA SCOTT is a digital archivist and content specialist with a master's degree in professional writing and publishing. She's a member of SFWA, and her work has been published in magazines, anthologies, and podcasts such as *Escape Pod, Gothic Fantasy: Agents & Spies*, and *Wild Musette*. Currently, she writes about the craft of world-building in her blog, Woman in the Red Room.

CHARLES W. WARREN has been a national newspaper journalist for more than twenty-five years. He lives in Surrey, southern England, with his wife, two grown-up children, and cat. He started writing short stories about four years ago and has had some success in competitions, and a number of his works have been published. He is delighted to see his crime story appear in the *TulipTree Review*.

WILLIAM HEMLEPP is a science fiction and horror writer living in Savannah, Georgia. He has been writing science fiction since childhood and strives to tell stories about real people through the lens of the fantastic. More work can be found on his Twitter, @WillHemlepp. This is his first publication.